"I *want* to kiss you."

Ethan kept his gaze trained on CJ's mouth as he spoke, shaking his head slowly from side to side. "I know it's wrong and stupid and impulsive and confusing, but the desire is there. I don't know how or why…" He breathed slowly as he closed the small distance between them, drawn to her as though it was the most natural thing in the world. He was still holding her hands, still touching her, and whether it was that combined with the pheromones surrounding them that propelled him to within the close proximity of her mouth, there didn't seem to be any force there to stop him.

"This is foolish," she managed to whisper right before his lips brushed a featherlight kiss to hers.

Dear Reader,

The bond between siblings is often a strong one, and this is the case with Ethan and Melody Janeway in my Sydney Surgeons duet. After Ethan goes through a tragedy, Melody encourages him to find a new path…one that leads him to meeting heavily pregnant Claudia-Jean in *Falling for the Pregnant GP*.

Claudia-Jean loves her town of Pridham. In return, the community rallies around her when she needs them most. Ethan comes from a large city, so it's little wonder he struggles at first with the way strangers chat with him. After a while, Ethan mellows and realizes not only the benefits of Pridham, but also the benefits of being around a wonderful person like CJ.

Likewise, in *One Week to Win His Heart*, Melody can rely on Ethan to offer sage advice when visiting surgeon George Wilmont comes into her life and turns it upside down. Melody is a strong woman who does her best to fight the attraction to George, but his open and honest manner wins her heart. George isn't sure what's happening when he meets Melody. It's as though she's jump-started his grieving heart. However, he doesn't know how to handle his feelings, nor the way he seems to be forgetting his first wife.

Sometimes being brave and taking a second chance at love can reward us with the utmost in happiness, contentment and, of course, wonderful families.

Warmest regards,

Lucy

FALLING FOR THE PREGNANT GP

LUCY CLARK

HARLEQUIN® MEDICAL ROMANCE™

Recycling programs for this product may not exist in your area.

ISBN-13: 978-1-335-66344-3

Falling for the Pregnant GP

First North American Publication 2018

Copyright © 2018 by Anne Clark

This edition published by arrangement with Harlequin Books S.A.

For questions and comments about the quality of this book, please contact us at CustomerService@Harlequin.com.

® and TM are trademarks of Harlequin Enterprises Limited or its corporate affiliates. Trademarks indicated with ® are registered in the United States Patent and Trademark Office, the Canadian Intellectual Property Office and in other countries.

Printed in U.S.A.

Books by Lucy Clark

Harlequin Medical Romance

The Lewis Doctors

Reunited with His Runaway Doc
The Family She's Longed For

Outback Surgeons

English Rose in the Outback
A Family for Chloe

The Secret Between Them
Her Mistletoe Wish
His Diamond Like No Other
Dr. Perfect on Her Doorstep
A Child to Bind Them
Still Married to Her Ex!

Visit the Author Profile page
at Harlequin.com for more titles.

To dearest Aunty Rae,
the road ahead might get bumpy but at least we
have each other to lean on.

Ephesians 3:12

Praise for
Lucy Clark

"A wonderful yet slightly emotional read in
this book, which hooked me from the very
beginning...I would recommend *Reunited with His
Runaway Doc.*"

—*Harlequin Junkie*

CHAPTER ONE

CLAUDIA-JEAN NICHOLLS STOOD on tiptoe, stretching as high as she could to the top shelf. 'Nope.' She relaxed back with a sigh and rubbed the large baby bump. 'It may help, little one, if you didn't continue to stab me with your elbows. Hmm? How about giving Mummy a break?' She stepped back to look at the item she wanted with longing. 'Why didn't I wear my platform shoes?'

'Do they make platform shoes that high?'

CJ turned to look at the owner of the deep voice but all she saw was a firm chest beneath a navy polo shirt. She lifted her chin to meet the man's gaze and saw a small grin on his lips. 'Are you teasing me about my height?' she asked, her tone light and jovial. When you lived in a small country town, it was almost second nature to have a chat with anyone you met, even if they were a stranger.

He shook his head, his grin widening. 'Not at all. Merely posing a question.'

'Well, to answer your question, no, I don't think they do.' Her own smile increased and she pointed to the item on the shelf that was out of reach. 'Would you mind helping me, please? Coffee beans. The red bag.' She placed a hand on her belly. 'There are a few at the back but how they expect me to get them in my condition is beyond me. I should demand a step stool for every aisle.'

'Or enlist the help of a tall friend every time you want to go shopping,' he offered. 'A safer option to platform shoes and step stools, especially in your condition.' He quickly obliged, obtaining the coffee for her. 'How tall *are* you?'

'Five feet, two inches tall and thirty-five weeks wide.' CJ chuckled at her own joke as she placed the coffee beans into her disorganised grocery trolley. 'Thank you for your help.'

'You're more than welcome.'

With another smile in his direction, she pushed her trolley a little further down the aisle, looking for the next item on her list. She could feel him still watching her and when she looked over her shoulder, almost hitting herself in the face with one of her blonde pigtails, she saw him frowning and looking down the otherwise empty aisle. 'Something wrong?'

'Er…no.' He looked up at the sign above them. 'This is aisle eight.'

'I know.'

'It's just I was told by the store manager that I'd find Dr CJ Nicholls in aisle eight.'

'And you did.' CJ spread her arms wide. 'And then you helped her get coffee beans from a high shelf.'

The man did a double take. *'You're CJ Nicholls?'*

'I am.'

'But…but…you're…er…too young.' At her arched eyebrow, he quickly continued. 'What I mean is…you look about eighteen years old.' He shook his head, his wide grin returning. 'You're having a laugh, right?'

'You think I look eighteen? How very flattering but add at least another twelve years to that and you'll be right on the money.'

'You're thirty!' The incredulity in his tone should have been flattering.

'I guess wearing my hair in pigtails doesn't help the argument that I am indeed a qualified general practitioner. It's just that wearing my hair up gives me headaches, keeping it loose makes me hot, and I really don't want to cut it so…' She allowed her sentence to trail off as she held out her hand. 'Claudia-Jean Nicholls. *Dr* Claudia-Jean Nicholls. I went to medical school and everything.' Her smile was wide, bright and absolutely dazzling. Her green eyes twinkling with merriment.

'Uh… Ethan Janeway.'

'Oh, you're Ethan.' She shook his hand enthusiastically, ignoring the small wave of heat that spread up her arm at the touch. 'I wasn't expecting you until this evening.' She gestured to her shopping trolley. 'Hence the reason for this last-minute shop. There's nothing in the cupboards.' Why, all of a sudden, did she feel so self-conscious? Perhaps it was because she was faced with a very tall, very dark and *very* handsome stranger who had the most amazing blue eyes she'd ever seen. A stirring of something foreign sizzled in her tummy and it definitely wasn't indigestion! He frowned and she flicked her pigtails back over her shoulders. 'Problem?'

'Why should it matter if there's nothing in the cupboards?'

CJ shrugged and glanced at her watch. 'Whoa, look at the time.' She started pushing the trolley and was pleased when he fell into step beside her. 'I guess I like to eat food when I get home from work,' she remarked, answering his previous question. 'I naturally presumed you would, too.'

'I don't follow. Why should you be concerned with where and when I eat?'

'Your lodgings, while you're in town, are at my house.'

'They're…what now?'

'I thought you knew. It was in the paperwork I sent through. We share a kitchen, laundry and lounge room.'

'The paperwork stated that accommodation was provided with the job. It's why I'm here.' He indicated their present surroundings. 'I went to the clinic to pick up the key for my lodgings, only to be directed here and told to find you.' His gaze rested momentarily on her pregnancy. 'I'm the locum to cover…maternity leave.' He spoke the last two words slowly, as though finally realising that she was the person he was locum for.

'That's right. I'm going on maternity leave as soon as we've got you settled, although why Donna doesn't think I can work up until—' She stopped. She and Donna had had several discussions about this maternity leave, namely that CJ didn't think she needed to take leave at all. Decreasing her workload to part time would have worked just fine but Donna had stood her ground and insisted CJ employ a locum. CJ had finally agreed to find someone for three months, Donna had insisted upon six months. 'Never mind. Any other questions?'

'Er…do we share a bathroom?' He glanced once more at her pregnant belly.

'No.' Her smile broadened. 'Which is just as well because, with Junior jumping up and down on my bladder all night, I need a clear path.'

'And that's why you're shopping? Because I'll be living with you?'

'Sharing a house,' she corrected. 'The bedrooms, with en suites, are at opposite ends of the house. We only finished the renovations last week.'

'You and your husband?' A small frown puckered his brow. 'Or partner?'

CJ dropped her gaze to her ringless fingers.

'My husband passed away. It's just me and the baby now.' She flicked a pigtail over her shoulder.

'I'm sorry. I didn't mean to be…indelicate.'

'You weren't to know and, besides, Pridham is a very small town. I'm sure you'll know all there is to know about me from the patients by the end of your first week.' She grinned. 'At any rate, the "we" I was referring to was myself and Brett, the builder.' She turned into the next aisle and checked her list again, then looked at the shelves and lifted a hand dejectedly.

'Why is everything on the top shelf today? I swear it's a conspiracy to stop pregnant women from getting what they want. Ethan, would you mind getting that jar of pickles down, please?'

'Cravings?'

She grinned again. 'Oh, yeah. Pickles and bananas are high on the list at the moment.'

'Your body must be low in sodium and potassium.'

'Excellent deduction, Dr Janeway. If I hadn't already been impressed with your extensive résumé, I am now.' She chuckled as she added a few more things to the trolley, checked her list and nodded. 'That's it…unless there's something you'd really like or need?'

He scanned the contents of the trolley before shrugging. 'I can come back tomorrow if need be.'

'OK.' She headed for the checkout.

'Ah, I see you found her,' Idris, the store manager, said as CJ started to unload the contents of the trolley.

'In aisle eight, just like you said.' Ethan quickly took over unloading the trolley, especially when she picked up a large tub of ice cream and almost dropped it. 'Allow me,' he stated.

'It's OK. I can manage.'

'I have no doubt but still, this one time, allow me.' Ethan continued to put the groceries onto the checkout conveyer belt. 'I thought, as you're almost to term, that you would have given up work a while ago.'

'Ah…the life of working in a small town. It's definitely a vocational calling because it's all work and no play. Plus, it's usually very difficult to get locums to agree to come this far away from a major city for any extended period of time.'

'I did.'

'Which means you're rare and valuable.' She smiled at him as he finished emptying the trolley. 'Thank you. It's also nice to meet a true gentleman.'

'Do you mean because I helped a pregnant woman?' He shook his head. 'That's not what makes me a gentleman because in my opinion *anyone*, male or female, should help a pregnant woman, especially one in her last trimester.' There was a slight vehemence to his words that

CJ admired. When her phone rang, she pulled it from her pocket. 'Dr Nicholls.' Her words were absentminded, still thinking about what Ethan had said, but her mind quickly cleared as her practice manager's voice came down the line.

'Just a heads up, CJ. Ethan Janeway's arrived. He came to the clinic to collect the key to the house and I told him you were at the supermarket. Did he find you?'

'Yes. Yes, he found me. We'll head back to the house so I can put the shopping away and then come over to the clinic. Nothing urgent?'

'No. Just wanted to make sure you'd met our new locum.'

'OK. See you soon.' CJ disconnected the call and paid for her groceries, watching Ethan put the bags into the trolley and begin to push it outside. He was definitely considerate. Hopefully that was a good sign that he would fit well into the town, the medical practice and the shared accommodation.

'Where's your car?'

'Over there.' She pointed to the silver Mercedes.

'Nice wheels.'

She shrugged. 'Not really my kind of car. It was my husband's,' she explained. 'It gets me from here to there and, at the moment that's all that counts.' They unloaded the shopping...well, Ethan unloaded the shopping, glaring harshly at

LUCY CLARK

15

her when she attempted to lift a bag. 'I used to walk most places but now…' she rubbed the heel of her hand over a part of her abdomen, pushing gently on the little foot that was underneath her ribs '…it's kind of impossible.' She took her keys out of her handbag. 'Did you walk or drive here?'

'Drove.'

'OK. Follow me in your car and we'll take this stuff back to the house.'

'Then to the clinic.' He nodded. 'I heard your conversation.' With that, he headed towards a red car parked opposite hers. The car immediately drew her attention. It was vintage with a soft top and leather seats.

'Wow! This is yours?'

'It is.'

CJ headed over to the vintage car and ran her fingertips lovingly over the rim of the door. The soft top was down, which gave her a complete view of the leather upholstered seats and wooden panelled dash board. 'It's in great condition.'

'I've had it restored.'

'Did you do it?'

'Most of it but my brother's a mechanic so I let him help.'

'Big of you.' She grinned and continued to walk around the car as she spoke, inspecting and admiring it as she went. 'May I have a quick look at the engine?' She'd come to stand before him, her green eyes glazed with an honest passion that Ethan found intriguing.

'Of course.' He lifted the concertina hood and stood back.

'Nice cams.'

Ethan was momentarily taken aback by her knowledge. He'd yet to meet a woman who understood cars. Now it appeared he'd met one—a pregnant one at that. 'Uh, thanks.' He scratched his head. 'How do you know so much about cars?'

'My dad. He used to restore them when I was a kid.' She shrugged one shoulder. 'I helped.' Her smile was still wide with delight. 'I think I should let you know that I *will* be begging for a ride or two while you're here.'

'Of course,' he said again. He lowered the hood and when she didn't say anything else, he gestured to her car. 'Shall we get going?'

'Yes. The ice cream's already started melting. Lucky it's not the height of summer.' He watched as she walked back to her car. What a unique woman. He shook his head as though to clear it from thoughts of CJ Nicholls—*Dr* CJ Nicholls, he corrected, who he'd discovered didn't look a day over eighteen, was heavily pregnant and had a passion for vintage cars. Definitely *not* the type of woman he was usually interested in, but she was definitely intriguing.

It wasn't the fact that she was pregnant that was presently bothering him, but the fact that they'd be sharing a house. Being around pregnant women wasn't his thing. He didn't shy away from them, and he'd proved that when his brother and sister-in-law had had their second child. He'd been the dutiful uncle, visiting in hospital, cooing and making all the right noises, but at the end of the day he'd returned to the peace and quiet of his apartment.

Living, for the next six months, in the same house with the temporarily pregnant CJ Nicholls and soon-to-be newborn baby wasn't what he'd signed up for. He wished he'd known the intricate particulars prior to his arrival because if he had, he wouldn't have come. Perhaps there was a hotel he could stay at, or an apartment he could rent, but both of those would take time to organise and would be exceptionally expensive.

He was still annoyed he'd been forced to take a sabbatical from the excessively busy hospital where he'd worked non-stop for the past six years. When he'd ranted and raved to his sister, Melody, rhetorically asking her what he was supposed to do with his time, especially as he'd finished working on his research project, she'd pitched the idea of being a locum in a quiet country town.

'It's four hours' drive from Sydney. You'll be able to breathe in fresh air, rather than city smog.

You'll be able to handle the work of a general practice with your eyes closed, and on weekends you can go for long drives in your car,' Melody had told him.

Ethan had to admit that the drive from Sydney to Pridham today had indeed been a relaxing one…at least after he'd managed to leave the city outskirts behind. Melody would be pleased he was trying to relax. His family had been worried about him, especially after he'd suffered a mild heart attack. 'A warning shot across the bows,' his cardiologist had told him. At least he was being proactive. At least he was trying to change by taking a break from his stressful job.

All of these thoughts went through his head as he followed CJ Nicholls's car back to her house…the house he was supposed to live in for six months. She drove carefully and responsibly, indicating with enough time for him to follow, and eventually she pulled into a driveway—with a double garage—across the road from the medical clinic and local district hospital. At least everything was nice and close.

Ethan helped her to unpack the car and carried the groceries into the kitchen, telling her to sit down and just point to where things went. CJ poured herself a glass of water and did as he suggested, lifting her feet to rest them on one of the other chairs at the table. He needed to gather more information, to find out whether there was anywhere else he could stay. Once the shopping was put away, he leaned against the bench and watched as she sipped her water.

'Ah. That's nice and cool.' She shifted slightly, rubbing her stomach. 'I could just curl up and sleep for a few hours.' Closing her eyes, she tilted her head back, exposing a long expanse of neck. Ethan swallowed, his gaze drawn to it. It looked soft and smooth and—

He forced himself to look away and cleared his throat. What on earth was wrong with him? He didn't do relationships, not since… He stopped the thought. Now was not the time to think about his past. 'Uh…so the house. Does it belong to you or…does the clinic own it…or…are there other places I could stay…or…' He let his words trail off and looked out the window next to the kitchen sink.

'You don't want to stay here?' Her eyebrows hit her hairline in surprise.

'Uh… I was just asking. I don't want to impose.' He indicated her pregnant belly. 'You're going to have your hands full very soon. Do you really want a stranger living here, cramping your style?'

CJ's answer was to take another sip of her water, clearly thinking over her words before she spoke. 'I have no objection to sharing the house. It's certainly big enough and I sincerely doubt you'll hear the baby crying all the way from your end. The walls are well insulated.'

'Part of your remodelling?'

'Yes. It's an old house but over the years I think I've gutted almost every room and redone it.'

'You like renovating?'

'I do. Houses. Cars. I like taking something old and making it new and functional, whilst at the same time still maintaining the essential character of the object.'

He nodded. He knew exactly what she was talking about because that's the way he'd felt about his car. 'You've lived here a long time?'

CJ nodded. 'The house was originally attached to the medical practice. The part you're in was the consulting area with a small emergency area out the back. The rest of the house was where we lived.'

'We? You and your husband?'

'No. My dad, my sister and me. I was thirteen when we moved in.' She grinned and he had to admit that when she did, it lit up her face. 'It was an old place but one we filled with love.' CJ rubbed her stomach, her words nostalgic and melancholy. 'We moved here after Mum had passed away. This town was our new beginning and that's exactly what we got.' She sipped her water. 'Five years later, the clinic across the road was built but Dad kept that part of the house…' she pointed in the direction of what would be his living area '…for his study, and the little surgery at the back became his bedroom.'

'Has he passed away?'

CJ nodded. 'Last year, after a three-year battle with Alzheimer's. He stayed here as long as he could before my sister found a great care facility in Sydney close to where she lives, and I stayed here to continue running the practice.'

'Is that what you wanted?'

'That had always been the plan.'

'Your plan, or his?'

'Both.' Her smile was natural and instant. 'I love this house, I love the town, I love the people.'

'And your husband? Was he also a local boy, too?'

'No.' CJ finished her drink, then stood and took her glass to the dishwasher. 'We should get over to the clinic.'

'I didn't mean to pry.'

'You didn't,' she said with a shrug before walking out of the house, not bothering to lock the door behind her.

'Uh…do we need to lock up?'

She shook her head. 'Crime is low in the town but if locking the doors makes you feel better, then lock away.' She didn't stop walking as she spoke, only gesturing back to the door. Her bright, jovial tone had disappeared completely and her words were flat. He really hadn't meant to pry, especially as she'd been quite happy to chat about her family. At least he now knew the topic of her husband was off limits.

As CJ opened the door to the clinic and headed inside, she couldn't help but notice the way Tania's eyes turned all dreamy at the sight of Ethan.

'Hi, handsome. Good to see you back,' Tania openly flirted.

'Any patients for me this afternoon?' CJ asked, trying to shift the receptionist's gaze from Ethan to herself.

Tania snapped out of it. 'Just two.'

'How many does Donna have?'

'She told me not to tell you. Just see your two patients, do your ward round and go home to rest. You know that's what you want to do, CJ.'

She sighed. 'I guess. When's my first patient?'

'Five minutes.'

'Good.' She walked down the small corridor into her consulting room, pleased that Ethan had followed. 'Did you meet Donna when you came in earlier? She's my partner.'

'No.'

'OK. Then I guess you haven't been shown around so I'll do that once I'm finished with the patients. You may as well sit in, start to learn the ropes.'

'Agreed.'

CJ sank down into the chair and sighed. 'I am

getting more tired than normal and that frustrates me.'

'You're so used to being busy?' He could certainly relate to that.

'Yes. Come Monday, you'll be taking over my consulting work. I'll be doing house calls with you this weekend…and maybe the odd one here and there over the next few weeks if it's OK with you. I just don't want to get bored and I know I will.'

'Was it Donna who insisted you get a locum to cover your maternity leave?'

'Donna, Tania, the nurses, the patients and the majority of the town. Yes.' CJ couldn't help the sad sigh that escaped her. 'I feel so useless and it makes me think back to when my father's health began deteriorating. *I* was the one trying to pick up the slack and take over from him without him realising it, but of course he did and—' She stopped talking and sighed again. 'I just feel big and useless and…fat.'

'You're not fat. You're having a baby,' Ethan calmly pointed out. 'And you're not useless. Your body is growing a human being! You studied anatomy, you know how difficult that is—to grow a human being. *I* can't do it. You can, so how about, as my first act as locum to this practice, I advise you not to be so hard on yourself and your temporary limitations.'

His warm, smooth words washed over her in

such a relaxing fashion that she felt her earlier tension begin to melt away. 'I suppose you're right.'

'I *know* I'm right.'

She smiled at that. 'Well, I'll accept the advice, even though you don't officially start consulting until Monday.'

'That's very big of you, Dr Nicholls.'

'I thought so.' The phone on the desk rang and she picked it up. 'Yes?'

'Jed's here,' Tania said down the line.

'OK. Send him in,' CJ replied before hanging up. Then she pointed to the phone. 'This is an internal line—usually Tania or Donna—and these two lights are your outside lines.'

'Always good to know. So, who are we seeing first?' Ethan stood and came closer, leaning over and pressing a button on the computer, pleased when Jed's file came up. 'Good. The same computer programme I'm used to.'

'Great. Sometimes it's the little things that can trip us up.' Like the way his spicy scent seemed to wind its way around her senses. It was nice. She liked it. She momentarily closed her eyes and gave herself a mental shake. That was the hormones speaking. Spices smelled more vibrant to her and she liked it. As Ethan moved back to his chair, ready for the consultation, CJ reset her mind where her new colleague was concerned.

Sure, he might be good looking and, yes, he

smelled wonderful and had gorgeous eyes…
and was tall enough to help her out when she
needed it, but he was just a locum…just a man
who would be out of her life in six months' time.
She shouldn't get attached.

When Jed came into her consulting room, CJ
smiled brightly and introduced Ethan. The two
men shook hands and when Ethan closed the
door behind Jed, CJ smiled her thanks then focused on her patient.

After the consult, she quickly typed up her
notes about Jed's treatment on the computer.

'Do you usually go out to the waiting room
and call the patients through?' Ethan asked.

'Usually, but at the moment, getting up and
down is difficult so Tania rings through when
the patients have arrived and I tell her when to
send them in.' The phone on the desk rang, the
light for an internal call blinking.

'I'll go,' he stated. 'What's the patient's name?'

'Chandra.' And before she could say another
word, Ethan had disappeared to the waiting
room, returning a moment later with four-year-
old Chandra and her mother. His actions, although well meant, only made CJ feel like an
expectant whale once more. She knew it wasn't
for ever and she knew that part of the way she
was feeling was due to her overactive hormones
but…she still didn't like it.

Once Chandra and her mother had left, Ethan

watched as CJ quickly typed the notes into the computer. Before she could finish, though, a sharp pain gripped her abdomen and she moaned, feeling very uncomfortable.

'What is it?' Ethan was instantly by her side, his gaze roving over her, visually checking for signs of labour.

CJ shoved away from the desk and stood up, walking back and forth as she rubbed the side of her belly. 'It's nothing. Just a swift kick from junior to mother. Ugh. I swear this kid is going to be a footballer.' She rubbed her stomach again and when the baby responded, without thinking she reached for Ethan's hand and pressed it to her stomach. 'See? Feel that? As a fellow doctor, you have to agree that that's one strong kick!'

When he didn't answer, she looked up. Their gazes locked and the atmosphere around them seemed to zing with newly charged electrons. Even deep inside her she felt them explode and she sucked in a ragged breath. It was unusual, it was unexpected and it was most certainly unwanted.

Ethan was stunned by the sensation. Not only was he alarmed by feeling her baby kick, a sensation he hadn't felt for quite a number of years, but also he hadn't expected the jolt that had travelled up his arm and ripped through his body. He was attracted to this woman! How was that possible? There was no way an attraction to anyone was paramount at the present time.

It took a few moments for him to realise she'd released her hold on his wrist. Still, he left his hand on her stomach for a fraction longer before jerking away and walking briskly from the room.

CHAPTER TWO

ETHAN OPENED HIS eyes and stared at the ceiling, furious with himself for not being able to sleep. Why had she put his hand on her belly? Feeling an in utero baby kick had been the last thing he'd wanted to do. It was also the last thing he wanted to think about right now.

He sat up, swinging his legs to the floor, then slowly looked around the room, lit by veiled moonlight. The wardrobe had sufficient coat hangers at one end and ample drawer and shelf space at the other. There were also several fluffy bath towels on one of the shelves.

In the corner of the room was an Australian jarrah desk, with a comfortable chair pushed beneath. The desk was functional but also kept with the decorated theme of the room, which, he had to admit, was very masculine. Well, CJ had mentioned that this part of the house had originally been her father's. Ethan looked more closely at the three framed pictures on the wall, which were all of vintage cars. Nice cars, too. Were they her father's pictures? Was that her father's old desk? If so, it leant a more personal touch to the room and he felt privileged she had chosen to have her memories on display for others to share. Perhaps seeing her father's things around also helped her to cope with the loss.

He hadn't done that. When he'd suffered great loss, he'd arranged for movers to come to his house and pack everything into boxes before delivering it to a storage locker…a storage locker he still paid for six years later. Then he'd sold the house and bought a sterile apartment near St. Aloysius Hospital. If he hadn't been forced to take time off, he'd be there right now, working and forgetting his past.

Sighing, Ethan raked both hands through his hair, keeping his thoughts on a tight leash. He *was* here, which was far better than lying on some beach, being bored for six months. As he took another look at the pictures, peering closely at the detail of the cars, he had to admit that CJ had gone to a great effort to make him comfortable, but what type of woman liked vintage cars?

He supposed a lot of women did but he'd never come across them before. It was a refreshing change. The restoration of his car had been a bone of contention between himself and Abigail. She'd accused him of spending more time with the car than with her.

'I don't mind you being at the hospital until all hours, Ethan. That's your job, I get it. But when you're home, I want you to spend that time with *me*, not your car.'

He stood and started pacing around the room.

He still felt uncomfortable about sharing accommodation with CJ. He wasn't used to living with anyone and he wasn't sure he wanted to adjust. He liked his life the way it was…or the way it had been before his imposed exile from the hospital.

Why had his body betrayed him like that? A prime candidate for a major heart attack? The medical tests had to be incorrect—even though he'd insisted the results be repeated. He exercised. He ate right. Sure, he was stressed but everyone else he knew was also stressed and they hadn't been told by the CEO to take a six-month sabbatical and de-stress. Why had it been—?

His thoughts halted as he heard a sound nearby. A door being opened and then closed? He strained, listening for more sounds. Quiet footsteps. Was there someone in the house? He shook his head, reminding himself that he was now *sharing* a house with someone else. Was CJ up or was there someone at the front door? An emergency? Did she need help?

He quickly pulled on a T-shirt, his legs already covered by a pair of pyjama pants. Deciding this was still too informal to greet a possible intruder, he grabbed his robe, belting it loosely before opening his bedroom door. When another sound came, he decided to go and investigate, his entire body alert. He crept into the hallway, keeping to the shadows as he made his way towards the kitchen. Peering around the doorway, all the tension left him as he saw CJ standing in front of the open fridge door, peering inside.

'Couldn't sleep?' he asked, walking into the room.

She jumped sky high and spun to face him.

'For heaven's sake, don't go creeping up on me like that.' CJ placed one hand over her heart and the other on the baby. She grinned at him and flicked her loose, golden hair over her shoulder. 'Although, if I do go over my due date, you could always scare me into labour.' She returned her attention back to the fridge and pulled out the pickles and bananas. As she moved, Ethan took stock of what she was wearing. She was dressed in an oversized nightshirt, her robe open and hanging down her back, and pink fluffy slippers on her feet.

'Baby won't settle,' she offered by way of explanation as she put the food onto the table. 'Would you mind getting the chocolate spread down from that cupboard, please?' She pointed in the direction of one of the high kitchen cupboards before turning back to the fridge. 'Want anything?' She pulled out a large bottle of ginger beer.

'No.' He put the chocolate spread on the table. Her silky hair was cascading smoothly over her shoulders and the urge to run his fingers through it surprised him. It had been a long time since he'd had such an urge, and he instantly quashed it. He'd met his first love at university, sweet Abigail. He ignored the surge of guilt that always came whenever he thought about her. Why, oh, why hadn't she let him help her? He clenched his jaw. Nothing could be done to change the past. He was done with love. Over. Gone. Finished.

Living here wasn't what he wanted. He didn't want to be around people, having to deal with emotions. He didn't want to be attracted to anyone. He didn't want to make compromises in his private life and if he'd had any doubts before, seeing his pregnant colleague shift around the kitchen only emphasised that he needed to live somewhere else.

'Keep me company,' CJ suggested, as she put a plate and knife on the table before easing herself down into the chair. 'Whew. I tell you, just getting up and down now is such an effort. I'll be glad when this is all over.'

'You'll still have to get up and down to the baby,' he pointed out, as he pulled out a chair at the opposite end of the table and sat down.

'Sure but at least I won't be lugging him or her around with me twenty-four hours a day, seven days a week. The baby can sleep in the cot and I can enjoy having my body back to myself.'

'Except for feedings.'

'True.' She sighed. 'Donna told me the other day that so many women spend so much time focusing on the pregnancy that they give little thought to what happens afterwards. The feeding, the nappies, the constant alertness even when you're exhausted.' She took a sip of her drink, then remarked, 'I think I'll be good at the last bit. Being a doctor, I'm used to the odd hours and the constant demand for my time.' She reached for a pickle, before proffering the jar to him. 'Are you sure you won't join me?' Before he could answer, she smeared the pickle with chocolate spread and held it out to him. 'It's oddly delicious. Want to try?'

A bubble of laughter escaped before he could damp it down. 'Thanks, but, no, thanks. You go right ahead.' His new colleague really was like no other woman he'd met before. She was open, honest and sometimes he wondered if she filtered her thoughts before speaking them out loud. Still, it was a refreshing quality to be around. It was as though she was more than comfortable with who she was and she didn't care who knew it. Abigail had always been so conscious of adhering to the dictates of society that sometimes he'd been worried at her lack of confidence in exerting her own opinions and thoughts. Where his wife had never wanted to rock the boat, it appeared CJ was more than happy to jump overboard and splash around in the water.

Ethan rubbed his chin and sighed. It was wrong of him to compare the two women as they'd clearly had very different upbringings. Why he was comparing them at all, he had no clue. What he was conscious of, however, was the salty and sweet scents of what CJ was eating and within the next moment his stomach growled, betraying him.

CJ chuckled. 'Grab some food. Shut that growling stomach up.'

'It's OK. I don't like to eat between meals.'

'Between meals? Ethan, it's…what…?' CJ glanced at the clock on the wall. 'It's three o'clock in the morning and clearly you were wide awake, as I'm pretty sure I wasn't *that* noisy. Perhaps you couldn't sleep because you were hungry.' She waved another chocolate-smeared pickle in his direction. 'If this doesn't tempt you, grab an apple or whatever takes your fancy. Go on. Live on the edge. Eat something *between* scheduled mealtimes.'

Ethan listened to her, his smile increasing as she chatted away, teasing him with light-hearted banter. 'Does everyone in this town talk the way you do?'

Her answer was to shrug as she chewed her mouthful, then swallowed. 'You'll have to figure that out for yourself. As far as I'm concerned, we only live our lives by the restrictions we force upon ourselves.'

'And do you *have* any restrictions?' His stomach growled again and he was rewarded with another light tinkling chuckle from the woman opposite.

'I guess you'll have to figure that out, too.'

He had to admit she had a nice laugh. It was a lovely sound and as it washed over him, he breathed in deeply and relaxed a little. 'Perhaps I will have a piece of fruit.' With that, he stood and went to the fridge. 'You keep bananas in the fridge?' he asked a second later and again she chuckled.

'Why not? It stops them from ripening as fast.'

'Is that true?'

CJ swallowed her mouthful. 'I have no idea but it sounds as though it could be true. And speaking of bananas…' She reached for the one in front of her and began to peel it, pleased she'd managed to break through his defences. After he'd stalked out of her consulting room, she'd sat there confused. She wasn't sure where he'd gone, but as she'd had to go over to the hospital after finishing her measly clinic, she'd found him there, in a deep discussion with the Clinical Nurse Consultant. Together the three of them had done a round of the ward, with Bonnie, the CNC, introducing Ethan to the rest of the staff.

She watched as he polished the apple on his robe before taking a bite, walking back to the chair he'd recently vacated. 'You have a nice smile,' she stated, and he paused, apple poised for another bite, and glared at her. 'Sorry. I didn't mean to blurt that out but it's true. I hope I didn't make you uncomfortable.'

CJ shook her head as she watched him take another bite of his apple. 'My dad used to say that I had no filter, that what I thought was what I said. Sometimes he said it was very refreshing and other times quite annoying.' She chuckled and took another bite of her banana. Life was what you made it and as far as CJ was concerned, she didn't have time for double talk and silly games.

'So…how do *you* handle it when someone just blurts out the truth, perhaps saying something you don't want to hear?'

'Huh.' She laughed without humour. 'My husband used to say a lot of things I didn't want to hear.'

Ethan nodded. 'I think that happens in most relationships.' At least, it had for him. There were things he'd regretted saying to Abigail and things he regretted *not* saying to Abigail. She, however, had preferred to keep quiet, had preferred not to tell him what was really going on in her life… even though he had kept asking her if something was wrong. She'd been so secretive. And too late he'd understood why. He slammed the door shut on his thoughts yet again.

'Well, in my marriage…' She hesitated for a moment, then continued. 'I may as well tell you because you'll no doubt hear my sad tale from the gossips in town.'

'You don't have to.'

'I'd rather you hear it from me, without the added embellishments. You see, my husband was having affairs. I, of course, was the last to know.'

'That...er...would have been...devastating.' Ethan shifted uncomfortably in his chair and took another bite of his apple.

'I guess I'd known our marriage wasn't working for some time as we rarely spent time together.'

Ethan's gaze momentarily dropped to look at her pregnant belly before meeting her eyes again, the lift of his eyebrows stating he believed otherwise.

'Well...clearly we spent *some* time together, but it was the *last* time as well.' CJ suddenly realised she was full and put the lids back on the food jars in front of her, just like she'd put the lid on her marriage, and shoved those memories back onto the shelf.

'You're very open, very trusting,' Ethan blurted. 'I've never met anyone like you before, CJ.' He put the apple down. 'I'm practically a stranger to you and yet I'm living in your home. Did you do any background checks on me? Did you research me?'

'Of course I did. I may try my best to be open and honest, as I find it avoids confusion, but I'm not naive, Ethan. I checked out your references and spoke to a few mutual acquaintances.'

'What? Who do we know in common?'

'I have several colleagues and friends at St. Aloysius Hospital.'

'Really?'

'Yes. I did my training there.'

'Huh.' He picked up his apple and took another bite. 'I didn't know that but, then, I know less about you then you clearly know about me. So, who do we know in common?'

'Carol Blacheffski. Steve Smith. Patrick Janoa. Melody Janeway.' She raised her eyebrows as she said the last name.

'You know my sister?'

She nodded. 'I know her well enough to ensure you weren't an axe-wielding homicidal maniac.'

Ethan sat up a little straighter in his chair. 'Wait a second. You know her? She told me she found the job in the classified section of a medical journal.'

'She did. I advertised for the locum then, as she knew me, she called me and we talked.'

'About me?'

CJ laughed and slowly started to ease herself up out of the chair. 'Clearly.'

'You both set me up!' He put the half-eaten apple onto the table and glared at her.

'How is this a set-up?' She spread her arms wide, as though she had no earthly idea what he was on about. 'I need a locum.' CJ gestured to her pregnant frame. 'The fact I was able to get a brilliant surgeon to come and cover my leave was a godsend. Trying to get a GP out here, in a small tourist town, for any length of time is bad enough as all the newly qualified doctors want to get their foot in the door at the big city practices and start earning the big bucks. You, on the other hand, needed some respite and to downsize your workload. Melody thought it was just what the doctor ordered.' CJ grinned at the pun.

'So you were organising me.'

'*I* wasn't. Your sister, on the hand, might have been. She sounded very worried about you.'

'And you didn't think to mention this to me earlier, that you knew Mel?'

'I thought you knew!' CJ spread her arms wide again before sighing heavily. 'It wasn't some big conspiracy and why does it matter *how* things transpired? The point is, you're here now and I'm very grateful.' Clearly Ethan was upset at this news but right now, with a small foot shifting awkwardly across her abdomen, she wasn't in the mood to have an in-depth conversation on the matter. She rubbed the baby, trying to ease the little one into a more comfortable position.

'Wait. Did my sister know I'd be sharing accommodation with you?'

'Uh…' CJ thought back to the conversation but her forgetful pregnancy brain made it difficult. 'I think so.' She shook her head and smothered a yawn. 'I honestly can't remember, Ethan, and

I'm tired now so I think I'll go brush my teeth again and head back to bed. Gotta be up in another three hours.'

'Actually, before you go, there's something I need to say.'

When she looked at him, it was to find him standing rigid in the middle of the kitchen, arms crossed over his chest. 'What's that?'

'Uh… I think it's best if I find somewhere else to live.'

'You don't like it here?'

'I don't like sharing.'

She pondered his words. 'That would have been interesting for you and your siblings while you were growing up.' It also rang some alarm bells in the back of her mind that she needed to watch her step where Ethan was concerned. Quinten, her husband, hadn't liked sharing things, except his bed. Quinten had also become overbearing and controlling. Was Ethan really like that or was that just the image he liked to convey so that people didn't question him too deeply? Either way, she had no room in her life right now for a drama king.

'That's not what I meant.'

'I know what you meant. You're not used to sharing accommodation. I get it.' CJ smothered another yawn. 'I don't think you'll find a furnished apartment in town available for the length of your stay. Most of the bed-and-breakfast places around here are booked up for the weekends and school holidays.' She rubbed her belly. 'However, you're more than welcome to try. If you're uncomfortable here and you feel that's what you need to do, then I guess that's what you need to do.'

'Just like that? You're OK if I go, even after you went to so much trouble to remodel your house?'

CJ hooted with laughter. 'I didn't remodel it for *you*.' She put the banana peel in the bin and stacked the dishes in the dishwasher.

'Uh…of course not,' he said. 'But is it OK if I stay here until I can arrange something else?'

'Of course.' After she'd finished tidying up, she headed to the door that led to her part of the house, but paused and turned to look at him. 'I'm guessing you're not used to being sociable and chummy with your work colleagues?'

'Did Melody tell you that?' He was annoyed with his sister and didn't disguise it.

'No. Your manner does.'

'Is that so?'

'Yes. It tells me that you're used to being respected, to not having your decisions questioned and that you don't particularly like interacting with subordinates.'

If he'd been uncomfortable before with the way she just blurted out her thoughts, it was nothing compared to now, and it was mainly because she'd hit the nail right on the head. In a matter of hours of their first meeting, CJ Nicholls had seen right through to the heart of him and it completely unnerved him.

'Ethan, if it makes you feel better, stay somewhere else and only interact with the staff and patients when absolutely necessary. So long as my practice is in one piece when I get back from maternity leave, I don't care what else happens.'

'I've upset you,' he stated.

'No.' She shook her head sadly. 'I'm not angry or annoyed, Ethan. I feel sorry for you. I thought we could be friends, but it's OK if that's not the case.'

'Look, Dr Nicholls, all I want for the next six months is to get out of bed, do my job and spend my evenings in peace.'

She stared at him for a long moment before nodding. 'OK. If that's the way you want it, that's fine.' There was no anger in her tone, no girlish outrage, but there was definitely a hint of pity, which was the last thing he wanted. 'Goodnight, Ethan. I hope you're able to sleep.' With that, she headed through the door that led to her part of the house.

Ethan stood in the kitchen for a while longer, pondering their conversation. He'd survived pity before. He'd been the source of gossip, people whispering in the corner, stopping whenever he walked by, then starting up again the instant he left. He'd locked himself away, just as he'd locked his belongings away and it had been working… until he'd met CJ Nicholls.

It really did leave him with one major question—should he stay, or should he go?

CHAPTER THREE

WHEN SHE WOKE on Saturday morning, CJ felt as though she'd been put through the wringer. She turned on her side, swung her legs over the edge of the bed and slowly pushed herself upright, keeping her eyes closed in an effort to stop the spinning sensation.

Gradually opening her eyes, she tried to focus but it was no good and a wave of nausea hit with force. She clamped a hand over her mouth and rushed to her bathroom. Once her early morning dash was over, she showered and dressed, beginning to feel much better, even though she was already exhausted.

'No one said the last trimester was easy,' she mumbled as she shuffled into the kitchen.

'Feeling better?'

She stopped. Ethan was sitting at the kitchen table dressed in a pair of casual trousers and navy cotton shirt, eating a stack of pancakes drowned in maple syrup. She sniffed appreciatively and smiled as she walked over to the stove.

'Yes, thank you. I guess baby didn't want the pickles, chocolate spread and bananas after all. These, however, smell delicious.'

'You still want to eat after…being sick?' There was concern in his tone.

'I do. Once the morning sickness has passed, I'm usually fine—' She chuckled. 'That is until the next time I eat something baby doesn't appreciate.' CJ peered at the pancake batter in the jug. 'So does this mean you know how to cook?'

'It does. Please, help yourself.'

CJ did just that and soon was sitting down with one pancake, drowning her own in real maple syrup. 'Mmm. These are heavenly, and if you decide that you do want to stay here for the next six months, feel free to make these any time.'

By now, Ethan had finished his breakfast and was stacking the dishwasher. 'Are you usually sick in the morning?' His tone was one of doctorly concern.

'No. Not really. I mean it depends on what I've snacked on around three o'clock in the morning.'

'That's your usual middle-of-the-night routine?'

'At the moment, but some advice I was given regarding children is that just when you think you've got them into a routine, they change it. So I'm not holding out because Junior here changes his, or her, mind almost as much as I do.'

'You don't know the baby's sex?'

She shook her head. 'I'm more than happy to be surprised.'

'And you've spoken to your obstetrician about your morning sickness?'

CJ angled her head to the side, surprised to hear the hint of real concern in his tone. 'You're concerned about me?'

'Naturally. You're a pregnant woman, I'm a doctor. It's part and parcel of who I am.'

She chuckled at that. 'I hear you wholeheartedly. I can't go to a restaurant without silently diagnosing the people sitting around me.'

'OK, then you understand that I'm only asking these questions because I'm professionally concerned?'

'I do.' She nodded. 'And although I know all the ins and outs of pregnancy and giving birth from a doctorly perspective, going through the process is giving me a whole new perspective.' She took a mouthful of pancakes, savouring the flavours. After swallowing, she continued. 'I've come to realise that my pregnancy doesn't run parallel to many of the medical texts but then, as Donna has said, each pregnancy is different and with mine, morning sickness has been sporadic throughout, not just in the first trimester. Even now, with only a few weeks to go, my appetite is as hearty as it's always been.' She smiled.

'And just to appease your concern, my blood pressure is fine, my ankles aren't swollen and I'll continue to see Donna weekly until the baby decides to make an appearance.'

'The obstetrician won't be here?'

'If she's here, then well and good but both Donna and I hold diplomas in obstetrics.' CJ forked in another mouthful.

'So you're happy for Donna, your friend and colleague, to deliver your baby?'

'Women in country towns usually rely on a friend or a grandmother or an old aunt to help them through deliveries, especially if it takes for ever for the doctor to arrive. Why is this any different? Except in my case, my experienced friend is also a well-trained doctor.'

'What about midwives? Are there any in the district?'

She shook her head. 'It would be good, though. We have two part-time district nurses, one from each hospital, but a midwife would definitely be helpful. However, the government believes that with two district hospitals and two GPs this area is well provided for…and I guess we're much better off than some other districts.'

He pondered her words as he fixed himself a coffee. 'Can I get you a drink? I see you have some decaffeinated coffee here. Or would you like some herbal tea?'

CJ shook her head. 'I'm fine for now, but thank you.' As she continued to eat, he hunted around the kitchen for the sugar and took the milk from the fridge.

He was glad she was receiving regular check-ups with Donna. With everything that had happened to Abigail, it had made his doctorly instincts almost over-cautious with all pregnant women. He would also need to get used to not working with the latest equipment and specialists on demand. He'd had no idea that Pridham would only have visiting specialists who came this way once a month, sometimes less, leaving the overworked GPs to pick up any slack. Perhaps this job was going to be more interesting than he'd thought.

Ethan glanced across at her, watching her devour those pancakes, secretly delighted that she was enjoying his cooking. He usually had little time to prepare balanced meals, preferring to grab something relatively healthy from the hospital cafeteria. Now that he was in Pridham, he would have the time to exercise more, do more cooking and drive his car. Sure, he'd be working but the stress would be different. Consulting in clinics and doing house calls would be very different from all-day operating lists, overbooked outpatient appointments, departmental administration work and research projects.

As he sat down to drink his coffee, he thought more about the conversation they'd had earlier that morning. It had unnerved him a little to discover that CJ knew Melody. Had Mel told CJ about Ethan's mild heart attack? Had she told

CJ the reason *why* he'd almost worked himself into an early grave? He sipped his coffee, glancing at her over the rim of his cup. Even if Melody hadn't said anything to CJ, had any of the other people she'd spoken to revealed gossip about Abigail? About the baby?

If she knew all about him, perhaps he should learn more about her? He'd called her trusting to take a stranger into her home but, likewise, he'd accepted a job and accommodation and had, for all intents and purposes, spent last night in a stranger's home.

What did he really know about the pregnant woman opposite him? She was a local in Pridham, ran a busy practice, held a diploma in obstetrics and was a pregnant widow. It made him wonder about her, made him want to ask more questions, to get to know her better, and that, in itself, was uncommon for him. He usually wanted to know as little about his colleagues as possible, other than they were competent and skilled enough to do their work.

Clearing his throat, he put his cup down on the table. 'Uh... CJ, if you don't mind me asking, how did your husband die?'

'Quinten died in a car crash almost nine months ago. It was six weeks after he'd passed away that I found out I was pregnant.' CJ sighed, shaking her head sadly. 'Quinten had never wanted children, anyway, so, regardless of the situation, I would have been raising this child on my own.'

'He would have left you in the lurch?' Clearly, from what she'd told him last night, her marriage hadn't been a happy one—at least near the end of it. He could relate to that far more than she probably realised. He and Abigail had been very happy in the beginning, but near the end…

She shrugged one shoulder. 'Who's to say? Perhaps he would have done the right thing and at least financially provided for the baby.' CJ put her knife and fork together on her plate, then leaned back and rubbed a hand over her stomach, smiling at her baby bump. 'Did you enjoy that, my sweetheart? Because Mummy certainly did.'

'How long were you married?'

'Five years, but we'd grown apart, as I mentioned last night.' She shrugged the words off with feigned nonchalance. 'That was my old life. I now have a new one I need to concentrate on.' She smiled brightly—a little too brightly, he thought as she levered herself up. 'Thanks so much for breakfast. Donna's doing morning clinic so we don't need to bother with that, although you will be rostered on once a fortnight to work a Saturday morning.'

Ethan nodded. 'I re-read all the paperwork last night.'

'Right, well, how about I slip on some shoes

and then we can head off to Whitecorn District Hospital.'

'That's the other district hospital where I'll be doing a clinic once a month?'

'Correct.' She cleaned up the mess she'd made, wiping down the benches before heading into her part of the house. When she returned, she'd tied her hair back into low pigtails and added a scarf. 'Mind if we take your car?' She batted her eyelashes at him pleadingly and smiled sweetly. He couldn't help but grin at her efforts.

'Subtle.' They headed outside into the April sunshine.

'Well, I did warn you that I'd beg a ride.'

'Yes, yes, you did.' Ethan held the passenger door open for her.

'There'll be more traffic on the road today, being a weekend.'

'Tourists?'

'In droves, but it's great for the area.'

'Bad for the doctors?'

'No. We're only called in when necessary and poor Donna's been covering any emergencies for the past few weekends anyway. I told her it was no trouble for me to be rostered on but she likes to mother me.' CJ sank down into the comfortable, upholstered leather. 'Nice.' She drawled the word out on a sigh. 'Oh, this is *very* nice. How much of the internal restoration did you do yourself?'

'I didn't do the seats or the dash but I certainly banged out a lot of dints and hunted through old junk yards until I found just the thing I needed.'

CJ nodded. 'You've got to take your time. Restoring a car isn't something to be rushed.'

'I completely agree.' Ethan was astonished to hear the words coming out of her mouth as they were the same words he'd said to Abigail. However, his wife really hadn't understood his passion, much as he would have liked her to. 'You're the first woman I've ever known to enthuse to the point of obsession over a car.'

'What do you mean, to the *point* of obsession? I *am* obsessed. Just as you are.' She laughed and closed her eyes, enjoying the feel of the wind on her face. As they drove along, Ethan once again found himself breathing a little more deeply than before. His cardiologist would be pleased.

'You're not filling your lungs all the way,' Leo had told him when Ethan had insisted the results of his physical examination be repeated. 'You need to slow down and—'

'If you say *smell the roses*, I'll punch you in the nose, mate.'

Leo's answer had been to laugh. 'Ethan, we've known each other for decades. I respect you as a medical professional *and* as a friend, and it's because you're my friend that these test results concern me so much.' Leo had shaken his head.

'It's just a hiccup. I'll slow down. I promise.'

'But you won't. I know you and this "hiccup", as you call it, may have been a mild heart attack but it means others will follow if you *don't* change your lifestyle. To lose you to a massive heart attack that could easily be prevented—it's a no-brainer. My recommendation to the CEO that you take an imposed sabbatical for six months stands. Smell those blooming roses. Breathe the fresh air. Get out of the city. Get out of your comfort zone. Meet new people and learn to appreciate life again.'

'I appreciate life,' he'd growled, completely furious with his friend. 'It's why I'm a surgeon.'

'Appreciate *your* life,' Leo had clarified. 'Fill your lungs—all the way. Breathe as deeply as you can and enjoy the exhalations as your stress ebbs away.' And for some reason, since his arrival in CJ Nicholls's life, Ethan had breathed more deeply than he had during the past six years.

Perhaps he was jumping the gun a bit, saying he wanted to look around for somewhere else to stay? He decided to put a mental pin in the thought and just see what else unfolded. For the moment, the drive through the beautiful countryside, surrounded by the early changing of the autumn leaves on the rows of grapevines, was very relaxing.

'How does the tourism impact the hospitals

and clinics?' he asked CJ after he'd negotiated the car out of the main road of town.

She lifted her head and glanced across at him, her sunglasses in place, a scarf covering her hair. She looked very...nineteen-twenties chic. 'We have the odd emergency—burst appendix, perforated ulcers, that sort of thing. Food poisoning pops up every now and then. Of course there are coughs and colds and general ailments people don't think of during the week because they're so busy running around. Then they go away for the weekend, their bodies start to relax from the daily grind and they pick up the slightest bug or virus.

'Sometimes we have people involved in car accidents, primarily because they've been stupid enough to drink and drive, but thankfully we haven't had anything for a few years.' She pointed to the road ahead. 'Go left at the T-intersection. The hospital's just down the road there.'

As he indicated to turn, he saw the Whitecorn District Hospital and soon they were pulling into the car park. When he brought the car to a stop, she turned and grinned wildly at him, slowly removing the scarf and sunglasses.

'That was...exhilarating. Thank you.' Her smile was so genuine, as though she didn't have a care in the world. How could she be like that when she was heavily pregnant and facing single parenthood? He stared at her for a long moment, astonished how her smile seemed to light up the darkness around his heart. He didn't want to be moved by her. It was one of the reasons he not only *wanted* to keep his distance but seemed to *need* it as well. CJ Nicholls was…an enigma and one he didn't want to discover—or so he told himself.

Ethan opened his door and climbed from the car before walking around to help her out. He took both her hands in his and after she'd swung her legs around, she carefully eased herself from the convertible. 'Getting in is much more graceful than getting out.' She laughed, staring up into his eyes. And it was there, in that moment, that it felt as though the earth had stopped rotating, that time seemed to freeze, locking the two of them in a strange bubble of awareness.

Was it the curve of her lips or the brightness of her eyes that was capturing his attention? He still held her hands, and they felt small and vulnerable inside his own. How was she going to give birth and raise a child alone? Didn't she know that so many things could go wrong? He knew. He'd experienced all those things and the pain had been acute. For that split second he wanted to haul her into his arms, to offer protection, to let her know that she had to be sensible, to formulate a plan and account for all possibilities. Why he felt so determined to protect her, he had absolutely no clue.

He glanced at her lips, his gaze hovering there for a long moment…long enough for her lips to part, allowing pent-up air to escape. What was this…thing, this…awareness that seemed to encompass them? Her lips were so perfectly sculpted, as though they'd been made for him… just for him. How was this possible? How could he be so drawn to a woman who, up until a month ago, he hadn't even known existed?

'Are you all right, Ethan?' Her words were soft and filled with concern and he immediately flicked his gaze back up to meet hers. He saw her look down at their hands and it was only then he realised his grip on her hands had tightened.

'Sorry.' He let go and took a step back, shoving his hands into his pockets. He didn't want to have any emotions, protective, caring or otherwise, towards his colleague. She was worried about *him*? 'I'm fine. Just…er…wanted to make sure you were steady on your feet.'

'I'm good.' CJ gestured to the main entrance of the hospital. 'Shall we?' As she walked on unsteady legs towards the hospital, leaving him to secure the car, CJ tried to understand what had just happened. Apart from being completely mesmerised by his spicy scent and having tingles of delight shooting up her arms from where he'd held her hands, she'd also seen a powerful emotion cross Ethan's face—one of primal protection.

Why would Ethan—a man who barely knew her—want to protect her? Want to keep her safe? It wasn't just his protective instincts she'd sensed. The way he'd stared at her mouth had caused the tingles already flooding her body to re-ignite and burst into a thousand stars of awareness. There was no denying that Ethan Janeway was an exceptionally good-looking man but the fact remained that they were colleagues. Besides, this was hardly the most opportune time in her life to be considering any sort of romantic involvement. The only person she needed to fall in love with was her unborn child. No one else.

With her pep talk done, CJ pulled on an air of professionalism and introduced Ethan to the hospital staff. She introduced him to everyone they came across, even the domestic staff, which was something he found a little strange. In a large hospital, it was impossible to find the time to get to know *everyone*, yet here it appeared CJ not only knew everyone, she knew what was going on in their lives—and they in hers. He shook his head. The intimacies of small, rural towns were not for him.

'Was I right?' she asked Toby, one of the male cleaners, who was swinging a polisher over the floors. They had finally finished a very long tour of the twenty-six-bed hospital, CJ bringing Ethan up to date on every single patient, and were on their way out.

'Yes, you were, CJ. Molly bought some of that manuka honey you suggested, swirled it around her gums and, sure enough, the ulcers started disappearing.'

'I'm glad.'

Toby turned the polisher off, then pressed his hand to her stomach. 'How's our baby doing?'

CJ grinned widely. 'Just fine.'

'Not long now.'

'No. Not long now.' She waited patiently for him to remove his hand before continuing down the corridor. At the main entrance, Andrea, the clinical nurse consultant who had accompanied them on the round, met them.

'Now, you go get off your feet. I don't want those ankles swelling,' Andrea instructed sternly, then she turned her attention to Ethan. 'Make sure she rests.'

'I will.'

'Oh, no,' CJ groaned. 'Have you joined the over-protection brigade as well?' she asked Ethan.

'Leave him alone. We're all here to look after you,' Andrea stated. 'That's what family do.'

'OK.' CJ smiled and waved. 'I'll see you to-morrow,' she threw over her shoulder as she headed towards the door.

'Tomorrow!' Andrea's tone made CJ stop.

'Claudia-Jean Nicholls, you are *not* picking grapes in your condition. Does Donna know?'

'That I'm planning to go, like I do every year? Yes.'

'This year's a little different, CJ. You're in no condition to pick grapes.' Andrea waggled a finger at her.

'I doubt there's any risk of me overdoing things. I have so many of you watchdogs around, guarding my every move.' She compassed Ethan in her words and Andrea nodded.

'True.' Then Andrea placed a hand on CJ's baby. 'I'm positive it's a boy.'

'Donna has a betting pool under way. Make sure you register your vote. Date, time, gender and weight.' CJ yawned, then waved. 'See you tomorrow,' she said again, before heading out to Ethan's car. She secured her scarf and sunglasses and gratefully accepted his help with buckling the seat belt. It wasn't until they were on the main road heading back to her house that he started asking questions.

'You're going grape picking tomorrow?'

'Sure. Have you ever done it before?'

He shook his head. 'Can't say that I have. I prefer to drink the wine from a bottle once the entire process has been finished.'

'Leaving it up to the experts?'

'Something like that.'

'Doesn't take an expert to snip off a bunch of

grapes. Besides, it can actually be a lot of fun. I
think you'll enjoy it.'

'Pardon?'

'I said I think you'll—'

'I heard what you said, but why did you say it?'

'Because you're invited.'

'To where?'

'To the vineyard tomorrow.'

'What vineyard?'

'Donna and her husband have a few acres of
vines. Quite small, compared to the large com-
panies around here. Every year we all go and
help pick the grapes.'

'Isn't it a bit late? It's April. I thought the
grapes were usually picked in February and
March?'

'It depends on the vintage, when it was
planted, the weather—lots of things. The grapes
on Donna's property are ready now.'

'They don't have machines?'

'No. It's not set up for machines, so we pick
by hand.' CJ yawned again. 'It'll be fun…and
a good way for you to get to know Donna away
from the practice. I was sure you wouldn't mind
but if you really don't want to come…' Another
yawn, her words starting to get more sluggish
as exhaustion began to set in. 'And want to look
around for other accommodation, then that's
fine, too.' She paused before saying softly, 'I
guess.'

Was it his imagination or had she sounded
a little disappointed if he decided not to come
and help with the grape picking? She did make
a valid point, though. Networking in a less for-
mal atmosphere would help him to build relationships with his new colleagues. Donna was
a partner in the medical practice and it sounded
as though several of the staff from both hospitals would be there. Ethan knew the importance
of networking and reluctantly admitted CJ had
been right to suggest he attend.

When he glanced over at her, it was to discover
she was asleep. Her head was at a slight angle but
they weren't too far from her house. He drove a
little more carefully, ensuring he didn't take the
corners too quickly.

'We're here,' he announced after he'd stopped
the car in her driveway. He gently placed a hand
on her shoulder to wake her but he couldn't. 'CJ?'
Nothing. 'Claudia-Jean?' Still nothing. She was
out for the count. He climbed from the car and
opened the door to the house with the keys she'd
given him yesterday. There was no way he could
let her sleep in such an uncomfortable position
because it wouldn't do her or the baby any good.

Ethan slowly and carefully helped her from
the car but still she didn't wake up completely.
He placed an arm about her shoulders to help,
but when she sagged against him, he did the only
thing possible—he swung her into his arms.

She was surprisingly light, and placed a lethargic arm about his neck before snuggling in. 'You smell nice,' she murmured sleepily.

He carried her through her part of the house and into her room, placing her on top of the bed. There, she pulled off the sunglasses and scarf before snuggling into the pillows. 'Thank you.' The words were hardly audible but he appreciated them all the same.

He stood there, watching her sleep. She still looked about eighteen years old and he smiled to himself. Her hair had come loose from one of the pigtails and was half over her face. Ethan reached out and smoothed it back behind her ear, then jerked his hand away as though unsure why he'd even performed the action. What was wrong with him?

She was beautiful, no doubt about that. There was something different about her...something unique that was drawing him in, making him want to spend time with her. Relaxing. That was it. He found being in her presence very relaxing and once again, as he breathed in, he was able to fill his lungs. It felt good...and at the same time confusing. Why was it he found her so compelling?

He raked a hand through his hair, exhaling slowly. She liked vintage cars, she liked driving in them, she liked chatting with people and being a part of a community. He could see some similarities. When restoring a car, you needed to take your time, to choose wisely. Was that how CJ lived her life? Taking her time to make long and lasting friendships? If today was any indication, he would say that was a resounding 'yes'. Did he?

As soon as the thought came, Ethan pushed it away. He had a life—a life in Sydney that he would return to in six months' time. He would be cleared to go back to work and that would be that. He had close relationships with his sister, his brother and his parents…at least, he *used* to have a close relationship with them. The past six years had blurred from one day to the next and on each of those days, work had been his only constant.

'Make new friendships,' both Leo and Melody had told him. 'Take your time with things. Live in the moment. Try new experiences.' Wasn't that what he was doing? What he'd done today? What he was planning to do tomorrow? He could feel the world of CJ Nicholls starting to envelop him and he wasn't sure whether it was good or bad.

'Hmm… Ethan.' The word was whispered from CJ's lips as she sighed and shifted slightly on the pillows.

His eyes widened at the sound. Why was she moaning his name in such a way? And why did he like it so much? He riffled his fingers through his hair again and forced himself to leave her room…immediately.

This woman was dangerous. She was making him feel things he didn't want to, and it was starting to get to him.

CHAPTER FOUR

ETHAN HEARD CJ wake during the night but he stayed in his room. There was no way he was going through a repeat of the previous early morning rendezvous when CJ had made him smile, had made him relax his guard. He was still trying to understand his reaction to his new colleague, still trying to figure out whether he should move out of her home or...

'Or what?' He whispered the words into the quiet room, lacing his fingers behind his head as he stared at the ceiling. 'Stay around and help her when she has the baby?' It wasn't as though she didn't have a lot of help being proffered from her friends and colleagues. Everyone he'd met since arriving in the district seemed to accept CJ's unborn child as part of their family. In the beginning it had confused him a little but he had to admit it was definite testament to CJ's easy-going personality. She was both respected and loved by the people of this little town. In fact, he'd never seen such loyalty before.

'That's because you locked yourself away. Your heart and your emotions.' He sat up, swinging his legs over the side of the bed as he said the words. They weren't his words, they were his sister's, his brother's and his parents'. His family had been worried about him after Abigail's death, after the baby's death. They'd done what he'd asked—they'd given him time, but when they'd thought that time was up, that he should be talking about his feelings, he'd pushed them all away. The only problem with his family was that they hadn't allowed it.

'If you don't want to talk about it, fine,' Melody had countered one night after she'd tried everything she could to get him to go and see a psychologist. 'But don't think you can push me away. I'm your sister. I love you. I care about you. Deal with it.' And she'd been right. He was fortunate his family loved him and now he was starting to realise how horribly he'd treated them, especially during those first few years after the tragedy.

Being out of Sydney, away from the frantic pace of life he'd forced himself to live, was really giving him time to think. He didn't like to admit it, but he was also coming to realise that he'd ignored his pain for so long that it had actually affected his health.

'I don't want to die,' he'd told Melody the night he'd returned home from hospital. After his 'hiccup', he'd been hospitalised for a few nights as a precaution and when he'd been released, Melody had insisted on staying that first night at his apartment with him. 'I miss her. I miss the baby, even though I was only a father for less than a day.' Ethan had shaken his head. 'I don't want to talk about it and I don't want to think about it, but neither do I want to die.'

And it was then his sister had voiced the plan of coming here, of getting away, of doing something productive but relaxing with his imposed six-month break. The fact that he'd managed to breathe more easily in the past forty-eight hours than he had in the last six years was clear proof that being here was the right thing.

But was being near CJ the right thing? Why was he so concerned with her? With her unborn child? Why had he felt that overwhelming urge to protect her and her child? Was it just because she was pregnant and looked the picture of radiant health? Her blonde hair, her smiling eyes, her mouth that would easily quirk at the corners, a smile always at the ready.

Ethan breathed in deeply, then out again as he thought about her.

Being with her, hearing the sound of her voice, enjoying the small memories of her father that were scattered around the house, the openness of this woman was encompassing him and helping him to slowly unwind.

He opened the curtains and gazed out at the night sky, the half-moon providing slivers of light. Ethan lay back down in the bed, propping his head up on some pillows, staring out at the stars. He reflected on how CJ had worn the scarf around her hair in the car, about how she'd fallen asleep on the way back and how she'd sleepily murmured his name. Even though he wasn't sure why she had, he couldn't hide his delight that she'd been thinking of him as she'd drifted off to sleep. Why he'd been delighted, he wasn't one hundred percent sure, only that…it had been a long, long time since any woman had sighed his name in such a way and it gave a much-needed boost to his ego.

At six o'clock, he was astonished when his alarm woke him up. He'd slept and, apart from the slight crick in his neck, he felt fairly well rested. As he headed to the bathroom to shower, the hot water helping to soothe his neck, he felt determined to try and enjoy the day CJ had planned for him. Networking was good. Networking was necessary if he wanted to break into the tight-knit community of the town, and this would be the way to do it. The last thing he needed was to be ready to help out in the clinic but have no patients booked in to see him because they didn't trust him.

Walking into the kitchen, he was surprised to find CJ sitting at the table eating a bowl of cereal. 'Have you been up all night?'

She looked up at him and smiled that sweet and lovely smile he hadn't been able to stop thinking about. She shook her head as she chewed her mouthful of food. He had to admit that she looked glowing, in a pale green knit top with three-quarter–length sleeves, the colour making her eyes more vibrant. Her blonde locks were once again in pigtails, making her look vulnerable and…adorable. She swallowed, her smile widening.

'No. Not *all* night. Junior let me get some sleep because…today is grape picking day!'

'Do you really plan on picking grapes or are you going to sit and put your feet up and let everyone else do the hard work?'

CJ laughed, the sound settling over him like sunshine. 'Not you, too. You're starting to sound like every other over-protective person in this town. I might help out a bit but only with the vines at chest height. My brain hasn't completely turned to mush.'

'Glad to hear it.' He took the cereal down from the cupboard.

'You don't need to eat. Breakfast is provided and it's a lavish spread.'

He put the cereal away and looked at her bowl.

'Junior was hungry.' She grinned and carried her bowl to the sink. The black skirt she wore swished around her legs and she adjusted the hem of her top so it wasn't crinkled over her stomach. 'So, does the fact that you're up and ready to shake, rattle and roll mean you're coming grape picking with me?'

'Someone's got to keep an eye on you.'

'Ha. Trust me, Ethan. Everyone there today will be keeping an eye on me.'

'They really are protective of you?'

'Yes.'

'Because your husband died?' He knew he was probing but what she'd said about her husband yesterday had only stirred up more questions. She hesitated before nodding. 'Were they protective of you *before* your husband's death?'

'Of course they were.' She looked away and gestured towards her room. 'I'll just grab my handbag, then I need to stop off at the clinic to pack my medical bag and then we can go.' She effectively changed the subject by walking out of the room.

Ethan frowned, his dislike for her husband continuing to grow, which was ludicrous. The man had done nothing to him and up until a few days ago he hadn't even known of Quinten's existence. Still, every time he mentioned her husband, sadness came into CJ's eyes—a haunting sadness that indicated her marriage hadn't been a happy one.

When she returned, she was her bright, happy self and they went outside. 'I won't be a moment,' she said, heading over to the clinic. 'You can wait in the car if you'd prefer.'

Ethan walked beside her. 'Expecting some emergencies today?'

She shrugged. 'I know Donna will have a well-stocked emergency kit but I still like to have a bag packed, just in case. Besides, there's the usual ailments—cuts, scrapes, mosquito bites.'

'Mosquitoes?'

'Yes. Because the vines are constantly drip-watered, it makes shallow puddles that are an ideal breeding ground for—'

'Mozzies,' they said together.

She packed her bag, going over the check list twice before locking up the clinic and walking back to her house. 'Can we take your car again? It's a dream to ride in.'

'Of course.' He held the door for her before heading round to the driver's seat. 'If you weren't pregnant, I'd even let you have a drive, but the seats don't adjust all that well.'

'I'll hold you to that once the baby's born.' Once her scarf and sunglasses were in place, she gave him directions to Donna's house.

'What is that smell?' he asked, as they neared Donna's house. 'It's like…alcohol and…' He sniffed again, unable to pinpoint the smell.

'Manure,' she supplied.

'Exactly.' He turned into the driveway and followed it up the winding path.

'The vineyard owners have to save water where they can, so it's recycled into "grey water". Sometimes it can give off a bad aroma but it's worse after the grapes have been crushed.'

'And this is supposed to be fun,' he stated dryly.

CJ laughed as Donna's house came into view. 'Yes.' She waggled a finger at him. 'So make sure you enjoy it.'

The house was surrounded with cars parked at all sorts of angles and Ethan managed to find a space not too far from where the festivities were taking place. He came around and helped CJ out of the car, his fingers lingering a moment longer than necessary. It was enough to make her pulse jump into the next gear and start racing with anticipation.

'Thank you.' The words came out on a breathless whisper. She glanced down at the ground and cleared her throat before meeting his gaze once more and smiling shyly up at him. 'I'm not used to playing the damsel in distress but there's no way I can get out of the car without help—at the moment.' She tried to laugh off the feelings he was evoking, telling herself she was silly for even experiencing them in the first place. Look at her, for heaven's sake. What man would find her attractive now?

'I don't think you're a damsel in distress.' His blue eyes were intense with sincerity, his deep voice slightly husky and filled with promise. 'I think you're a radiant mother-to-be.'

She swallowed, unable to look away. They were standing closer than she'd realised and she could still smell the fresh scent of his shower. Everything around them became a blur as they continued to focus solely on each other. Desire—surprising yet very real—raced through him at an alarming rate and he forced himself to take a step away.

As he closed the car door behind her, CJ was thankful for the momentary reprieve as she tried to squash the emotions he was forcing to the surface. She cleared her throat. 'I'd better go find Donna. Would you mind passing me my bags, please?'

Once she had them in her hot little hands, she took off so fast he was surprised. The only time he'd seen a pregnant woman walk that quickly was when she needed to go to the bathroom! Perhaps that's where CJ was headed...or perhaps she wanted to get away from him.

Either way, he was very glad there was a growing physical distance between them. 'Just do your job and get back to your life,' he muttered to himself as he followed the direction CJ had taken towards the house.

'Yoo-hoo! Dr Janeway.' He turned at the sound of his name being called. He was just about to head up the few steps to the front door when Tania, the receptionist from the clinic, came around the side of the house. 'We're all out the back. Here.' She linked her arm through his. 'I'll show you.'

Ethan forced himself to smile as he allowed himself to be led by Tania. 'Look who's here,' Tania chattered as they came around the house to the rear entertaining area where about twenty-five people were gathered. There were introductions all around and before he knew it, an empty plate was being thrust into his hands and he was being guided towards a rustic table laden with food. There were cold meats, cheese, salads and loads of fresh fruit.

He was greeted warmly by Donna and her husband, as well as many others, and all the while he made polite conversation he kept an eye out for CJ. Was she all right? Was she inside with her feet up? He wanted her to rest but he also wanted to be around her. She was his anchor in this strange new place and he was a little miffed that she'd deserted him so quickly upon arrival.

Had she felt it, too? That tug? That stirring of desire that he'd experienced yesterday at White-corn Hospital but which he had brushed off as 'ridiculous'? Today, though, when he'd held her hand, when he'd stood close to her, when he'd breathed her in, he could have sworn she'd been just as mesmerised by him as he'd been by her. How was that possible? They barely knew each other.

'Try the olives,' she told him, suddenly appearing by his side, plate in hand. 'They're grown on the property, too.'

'You're hungry again?'

'Eating for two,' she stated, loading up her plate. When she went to sit down, he was pleased she'd left room for him to sit next to her. The conversations flowed naturally and after a while of feeling like an outsider, Ethan began to relax. These were nice, genuine people and they were accepting him as easily as CJ had.

Two hours later, the grape-picking had well and truly begun. Once he'd been shown what to do, Ethan worked quickly and efficiently. He was by no means a stranger to hard work and found the task both enjoyable and, oddly, relaxing.

'Having fun?' She pulled on one glove to protect both her hand and the grapes.

'Yes. I am.'

'You sound surprised.' CJ used her pair of snips and cut off a bunch of grapes, putting it into his bucket.

'I am.'

'Are you always surprised when you try something new and it turns out to be fun?'

He nodded. 'Leaving Sydney. Coming to a new town. Meeting new people.' He listed them. 'I didn't think any of them would be fun but it hasn't been as bad as I'd thought.'

'And what about sharing a house with another person?' she added, then looked at him questioningly. 'Are you going to stay?'

Ethan pondered her words for a moment. 'There's no denying that your place is practical. It's close to the clinic and hospital. That's a bonus. There's somewhere for me to garage my car. That's good, too.'

'You've heard me having morning sickness, seen me sleeping in your car and shared night-time snacks with me.' She ticked the things off on her fingers. 'I'm thinking that any other awkward moments we might share would pale in comparison to those.'

Ethan couldn't help but laugh at her words. He found her openness completely refreshing as Abigail had rarely said what she'd been thinking. That had been part of their problem. He'd allowed himself to think she was fine and… He focused his thoughts on the woman before him, rather than his past. 'You really are the most unique woman I've ever met.'

'I'm going to take that as a compliment.'

'You should.'

And there it was again. They were looking at each other with a strange sort of awareness, as though an invisible bond was forming between them. His gaze dipped down to encompass her mouth and watched as the smile disappeared, her tongue slipping out to wet her lips.

'Thank you,' she said quietly.

'For…?'

'For saying nice things like that—and meaning them.'

'You're not used to receiving compliments?' He waved an arm around at the various people who were picking grapes. 'Everyone I've met in this town simply adores you.'

She chuckled. 'But most of them have known me since I was a young girl.' She went back to snipping grapes and so did Ethan. 'When I first started working in the practice with Dad, I used to think the respect I was given was by association. They respected my father, so they were giving me the benefit of the doubt.'

'And now?' Ethan crouched down to snip the lower bunches of grapes.

'I know they respect me because I'm a good doctor and also because of the way I loved and respected my dad.' CJ gestured to where some other people were cutting grapes a few rows away. 'Take Robert, for example. He knew my dad, helped him restore cars, played darts with him and it wasn't until my dad's funeral that Robert told me how proud he was of me. Proud that I'd become a great doctor, like my dad. Proud because as my father's health had deteriorated, I'd treated Dad with respect.' CJ sniffed as tears sprang to her eyes. 'It was nice to hear.'

'You clearly still miss your dad very much.'

'I do. Every day.' She smiled and snipped another bunch of grapes. 'I know the people of this town love me, which is one of the reasons I always refused to leave whenever Quinten voiced the idea.'

'He didn't like it here?' Ethan asked cautiously. He was willing to listen to CJ talk about her husband but he didn't want her getting upset. She'd already been standing on her feet for quite a while and although it wasn't summer, it was a warmish kind of day.

'He did at first. He came here from Sydney to start afresh after a bad business deal. We'd met, dated and were married within the year.'

'That's fast.' He thought about he and Abigail, being friends throughout university and eventually taking their relationship to the next level many years later.

'That's what everyone said but I was determined, and so was he. And things were great for the first few years. I think he had some notion that wherever he went with his work, I would follow. A business deal came up in Sydney and he was all gung-ho, ready to just up and leave.'

'But you couldn't. You're a country doctor with a busy practice,' he stated.

'Exactly. Dad's health had deteriorated, I was working round the clock at the practice and helping my sister move Dad to Sydney.'

'Perhaps Quinten thought you wanted to be closer to him?'

'That was one of the arguments he put forward. Quinten was very good at manipulating situations to his own advantage. Yet where he was planning on living in Sydney would have been a two-hour drive in peak traffic from where my father was.'

'It sounds as though—' Ethan stopped and shook his head. 'Never mind.'

'It's OK, I know what you're going to say and you're not the first person to say it. Quinten didn't respect me. Not as a woman, or as a doctor.'

'It does sound that way.'

'It's true. He told me that my refusal to leave and move to Sydney was what had ended our marriage for him.'

'Did he leave?'

She shook her head. 'The business deal fell through, which he blamed me for. He was always looking for that "get rich quick" scheme, and I eventually discovered the truth behind his initial move to Pridham in the first place. He'd lost a fortune on the stock market. Of course, at the time he told me it was something else, someone else's fault—never his. It was just lie after lie, and I was too naïve, as far as men went, and believed everything.' CJ snipped a large bunch of grapes with extra force. 'I'm not now. When you learn lessons the hard way, they tend to stick.'

'You're a strong, independent woman.' It was a statement and CJ nodded firmly.

'Damn straight.' She held her snips in her gloved hand and rubbed her belly protectively. 'I've got to be strong. The baby needs me.'

Ethan straightened and smiled. 'Good to hear.'

'Thanks for listening to me ramble.' She moved her hand around to her back and began rubbing in the arch.

'Thank you for trusting me.' He looked down at their bucket. 'I think that's full enough. Shall we take it in?'

CJ nodded and removed the glove from her hand. Then, as they walked back down the row of vines towards the house, she linked her arm through his, as though it was the most natural thing in the world. When Tania had done the same thing earlier, he'd been slightly uncomfortable. Now, though, when CJ did it, he found nothing uncomfortable about her touch, neither did he see anything in her expressive eyes other than happiness.

Had they just become friends? He wasn't used to making new friends this fast but perhaps that was because he usually held everyone at bay. Since Abigail's death, he hadn't let anyone new get close to him and yet as CJ had been talking he'd felt the urge to share his own story with her, to tell her of his own disastrous marriage so CJ would know she wasn't the only one who had felt so broken-hearted.

'CJ!' The urgent call came through the house.

'What's wrong, Tania?'

'Robert's been stung by a wasp and he's not feeling too good.'

'What?' Ethan was surprised. 'There are wasps around here?' They all headed for the door. CJ headed into the kitchen and rummaged around in Donna's cupboards.

'What are you doing?' Ethan demanded.

'Getting some pure honey. Grab my medical bag, will you? It's over near the table.' He did as she asked and once she'd found the honey they headed out.

'So why are there wasps?'

'When the birds peck the fruit, it makes them nice and sweet.'

'Perfect for bees and wasps.'

'There aren't too many about, wasps, I mean. Where's Donna?' she asked Tania as the receptionist led the way to where Robert had been picking grapes.

'She forgot the bratwurst so she's gone to the shops.' Tania led the way but when Ethan saw Robert, lying on the ground, his body beginning to shake, he ran ahead.

'He's going into shock.' Ethan felt for Robert's pulse and checked his breathing. 'Someone get a blanket and call the ambulance. Robert? Robert, can you hear me? It's Ethan.' The response he received was a whimpered cry. 'Did you know he was allergic?' Ethan asked CJ.

'No.' CJ was working quickly, drawing up a shot of adrenaline before handing it to Ethan. As he was crouched down near Robert, it was easier for him to administer it.

'Oh, Robert…' His wife, Amanda, dithered and CJ quickly comforted her.

'He'll be fine. I'm going to treat the stings and the adrenaline Ethan's administered will help settle things down.'

'Will he need to go to hospital?'

'I'd like to keep him in overnight just so we can keep an eye on him.' CJ slowly knelt on Robert's other side and opened the honey.

'Oh.'

'He'll be fine,' CJ reiterated.

'What? What are you doing?' Ethan asked as CJ glopped some honey onto the sting sites.

'The honey soothes the skin. It also helps reduce swelling and any painful sensations. How's Robert's pulse rate now?' She waited while Ethan placed his fingers to Robert's carotid pulse.

'Better.'

'There's a portable blood-pressure monitor in my bag.'

'Great.' He hauled it out and wrapped the cuff around Robert's arm before pumping it up to check his BP. 'It's low but the adrenaline should bring it back up soon.'

'How are you feeling now, Robert?' CJ asked gently.

'Sleepy.'

'OK, but I need you to stay awake, just for a bit longer. We're going to get you to hospital where you'll be pampered like a prince.'

'Whitecorn?' The question from Robert was weak.

'No. Pridham, that way you'll be nice and close to Amanda.'

'Amanda?'

'I'm here, darling.'

CJ watched as Amanda knelt down and bent to kiss her husband's cheek. Even at their age, they were still there for each other. CJ rubbed a hand over her stomach, making a silent promise that she'd always be there for her child—no matter what. She glanced up and was startled to find Ethan watching her. They shared a brief moment when they seemed to connect on such a personal level, then he returned his attention back to their patient.

CJ followed suit and concentrated on the stings. 'The swelling seems to be reducing,' she told Robert. 'Does it still hurt a lot?'

'I've had worse.'

Amanda's concerned laugh helped lift the mood. 'That's the spirit.'

'Ambulance is here,' Tania called.

Just before they shifted Robert onto the stretcher, Ethan took his blood pressure again and was happy to report it had improved dramatically.

'Told you you'd be fine,' CJ reassured Robert as the stretcher was manoeuvred into the rear of the ambulance.

Donna arrived home from the shops and was quickly being brought up to date on the situation.

'I'll travel in the ambulance with him,' Amanda said. 'Could someone bring my car to the hospital?'

'I'll arrange it,' replied Donna. 'CJ, you and Ethan go get Robert settled in and, Ethan—' Donna fixed him with a determined look '—afterwards I want you to take CJ home and make sure *she* has a rest.'

'Good call.'

'Here are your bags, CJ,' Tania said as she came running out from the house. She smiled at Ethan. 'See *you* tomorrow.'

Ethan escorted CJ back to his car after thanking Donna for a wonderful morning.

'I can drop you home first.'

'Pardon?'

'I can drop you at home first and then go to the hospital to see Robert settled.'

'It's all right. Robert might get worried about me if I don't turn up.'

'I'll tell him you're having a rest. It's what pregnant mothers do.'

'Still, I don't want to worry him. He likes to

fuss over me as his own grandchildren live too far away.'

'It appears most of the town of Pridham—and Whitecorn, for that matter—love to fuss over you.'

'Yes. It's nice.'

He could imagine it would be for her. She wouldn't take it for granted either. Instead, it was obvious she appreciated every single person's protective attitude towards her and her unborn child.

It didn't take them long to get Robert settled and once CJ was satisfied with her patient's vital signs, Ethan took her home.

'Off to bed, sleepyhead.'

'OK.' She stifled a yawn and shuffled off towards her bedroom. 'Wake me if anything exciting happens.'

That was the last Ethan saw of her for the rest of the day. He knew she'd wake up an hour or so later and specifically made sure he was out of the house. He went for a drive, enjoying the scenery and the ambience of the area. It was relaxing, colourful and a million miles from the hustle and bustle of Sydney.

When he returned it was night-time and again there was no sign of her. He went to his room and got ready for bed. He had clinic tomorrow morning and house calls in the afternoon. Although the pace was different from Sydney, the patients still had real complaints and he owed it to them to be alert.

He glanced over at the clock. It was only nine-thirty and here he was, tucked up in bed. If his colleagues could see him now, they'd laugh. Perhaps it was the manual labour he'd done that morning that was making him feel so exhausted. 'Or maybe it's the way you can't seem to get CJ out of your head,' he muttered, and buried his head beneath the pillow, forcing his thoughts in a completely different direction.

CHAPTER FIVE

Four-fifteen. The digital clock had to be wrong. He'd been tossing and turning for hours. *Surely* it was almost morning! He flung the covers back, climbed from the bed and pulled on his robe. He needed a drink, and not just water from the bathroom tap.

Ethan headed out to the kitchen, stopping in the doorway to check that the coast was clear. Had CJ been up already? He glanced around the darkened room. There were no signs that anyone had been in the kitchen. No jars of chocolate spread left out, no dishes in the sink. Perhaps she'd packed everything away in the dishwasher.

Regardless, the kitchen was empty now. Ethan hurried over to the sink and filled the kettle with water then switched it on. While he was waiting, he looked through the herbal teas CJ had in the cupboard, and decided on Sleepy Baby tea, as it prescribed a relaxing outcome.

Herbal teas had been a more recent addition to his 'new lifestyle' campaign. Melody had suggested it, saying that it often helped her to get a good night's sleep. 'You need at least six hours of REM sleep, Ethan.'

'I get six hours of sleep,' he'd argued.

'In one block?' Her questions had been pointed. 'Didn't Leo suggest you cut down on your caffeine? How many cups do you usually have?'

Ethan had shrugged. Most days he lost count but even he knew it was too much. He did what he needed to do in order to get through his day, being as effective as possible, and he said as much to his sister.

'But you're not being effective.' Melody had reached out and taken his hand in hers. 'Don't you see that? You may be keeping up to date with your paperwork, your research projects, and being a brilliant surgeon to your patients, but at the end of the day you're being ineffective to your own health.'

'I don't care,' he'd told her, the soft, caring tone doing more to damage his self-control than anything else.

'About your own life?' Tears had instantly sprung to Melody's eyes and it was then, seeing his sister's worry and concern, that Ethan had started to actually listen to her biggest fears for his health. He'd tried to change, tried to cut down on the caffeine, but about four weeks after that conversation his body had decided to take control of things by having a mild heart attack.

'Morning.' CJ's soft, cheery greeting startled him, and it was only then he realised that the memories had brought tears to his own eyes. Ethan quickly sniffed and turned his attention to finding a cup and putting the teabag into it. 'Junior's doing the morning exercise routine a little later today. Maybe there's hope.'

'For what?' Ethan glanced over his shoulder at her, noting she looked absolutely adorable with her hair all messed up and stuck out at funny angles. Her robe was hanging open and her feet were in those ridiculous fluffy slippers. She looked…good enough to eat. Ethan cleared his throat, willing the kettle to hurry up and boil.

'That Junior's going to grow out of being an early riser,' she answered.

Ethan's lips quirked slightly. 'Wishful thinking?'

She crossed both her fingers and held up her hands, making him smile even more. 'Something like that. What are you drinking?' She peered into his mug on her way past him to the fridge.

'Herbal tea.'

'Mmm. Sounds good.'

Without saying another word, Ethan took another cup down and added another teabag. 'Sugar or honey?'

'Honey, please.' She took some cheese out of the fridge and headed over to the bread bin where she retrieved a small baguette. 'Hungry?'

'No, thanks.'

She closed the bread bin, picked up a knife and a plate before seating herself at the table. 'So why can't you sleep?' She spread some cheese onto the bread.

Ethan looked at her, his mind filtering through several different things he could say. Thankfully, the kettle switched itself off and he almost pounced on it, pouring water into the waiting cups. 'Adjusting to a different place.'

She swallowed her mouthful. 'Miss your own bed?'

'Something like that,' he murmured. When the tea was ready he took hers to the table before walking towards the door with his own mug. 'See you later in the morning.'

'You're not going to stay and keep me company?'

She'd asked him that before and he'd stayed. Because he'd stayed, he'd become better acquainted with her. After their time picking grapes together, he would now say that they were becoming friends and if that was so, wouldn't that mean she'd want him to talk about his own life? Part of him did want to tell her about Abigail, to open up and be free from his self-imposed exile, but the other part—the logical part—wanted to leave the kitchen and find a way to return their relationship to one of strict work colleagues. However, it was *because* she was an open, honest, giving person, that he knew if he didn't stay, at least for a few minutes while he drank his tea, and keep her company, she might be offended.

'Sure.' He turned back to the table and sat a few seats away from her.

CJ blew on the hot tea. 'So, I called through to the hospital to check on Robert. He's sleeping soundly. All vital signs are fine.'

'Good.'

'I'm glad you were there to help.'

'You would have been able to handle everything with your hands tied behind your back,' he commented.

'Thank you. That's nice of you to say, but I have to tell you, in my present condition, I definitely can't move as fast as you. It's frustrating.'

'I'm sure it is. Soon, though, it will all be over—'

'And I'll be frustrated for a different reason,' she finished with a wry grimace.

'I thought you were looking forward to it.'

'I am. I'm getting desperate to meet my child. To hold it in my arms, to smother it with kisses, but the fact remains that being a single mother is not going to be an easy trick. Then there's the clinic and what if I need time off after you leave and we can't get another locum? What if something goes wrong with the birth? I'm happy with my level of medical care, don't get me wrong, but I just have all these thoughts constantly running through my head and I can't seem to stop them.

'What if I go over my due date and I have to be induced? What if I have a reaction to the medication? What if it's so painful I can't cope? What if Donna's at another emergency and I have to deliver the baby myself? What if something's wrong with the baby? Am I going to be a good mother?' Her voice had risen to a crescendo and she buried her head in her hands, her shoulders shaking as she started to cry.

Ethan was horrified. Not at what she'd said but how concerned she was about everything. He'd had no idea her stress levels were this high and the doctor side of him kicked in, knowing such stress could seriously affect her blood pressure.

'I was trying to call Donna to talk to her about all of this but she's actually out at an emergency at Whitecorn Hospital and I also don't want to bother her every time I have a moment of neurotic weakness. And…and…all of those questions are only the tip of the iceberg because once my anxieties start to warm up, they really get going.' She sniffed and raised her head again. 'What if I can't cope with the baby and can't return to work—ever? What if I have postnatal depression? What if I can't do this by myself?'

'Borrowing trouble won't get you anywhere.' He tried to placate her, wondering if he should leave a message for Donna to stop by after the emergency. For the moment, the best thing he could do was to let CJ talk, let her get her frustrations out, because he'd come to realise that she wasn't the sort of person to bottle things up…

unlike him. If she could talk things out, cry a little and release the pressure from her anxious thoughts, then she soon might be able to get some rest.

Tears continued to trickle down her cheeks and she patted the pockets of her dressing gown for a handkerchief. Trying not to feel helpless but also wanting to be helpful, Ethan quickly took the box of tissues from the window ledge and brought them over to her.

'Thanks.'

He sat down beside her and took her small hand in his. The instant he did that, he realised his mistake. His intention had been to talk to her like any other patient, to reassure her, but all he could now concentrate on was that her skin was so incredibly soft. Ethan rubbed his free hand over his forehead, trying to jump-start his mind. When he spoke, his voice was lower, more intimate than he'd intended. 'It's natural to have doubts, CJ. Very natural.'

'I know, but what if some of them come true?'

'Then you'll deal with them.' His words were direct and filled with hope. 'One by one. You'll formulate a plan, you'll find the help you need, and you'll get on with things. You're very well supported in this town. Everyone—and I mean *everyone*, from the cleaner at Whitecorn Hospital to the store manager at the grocery store—is supporting you.' He shook his head in amazement.

'I know I've said this before but it really does astound me because I've never met anyone who was so well respected and so adored by those around her. You're a genuinely nice person, CJ.'

'Wow.' Fresh tears trickled down her cheeks, but they were tears for a different reason. 'That is such a lovely thing to say, Ethan. Thank you. You're a good friend.' She withdrew her hand from his and blew her nose.

Ethan closed his eyes, remembering a very similar conversation with Abigail. She'd been stressing and he'd placated her, thinking he was comforting her, but he'd been wrong. Her worries had been well founded and he hadn't done enough to help, because she had kept so much from him, and he hadn't seen the danger till it had been too late. It was one of the things that ate him up at night and even though the specialists had told him there was nothing he could have done for either his wife or his child, deep in his psyche he couldn't stop feeling that hadn't been the case.

Well, he wasn't about to let history repeat itself. He'd managed to verbally reassure CJ but actions often spoke louder than words. 'Well, then, friend, why don't I organise an ultrasound for you? It'll help put your mind at ease. You'll be able to see that the baby is OK and I'm sure Donna can arrange a urine test if that will also help alleviate any concerns you might have.'

'Because I don't want my patients being seen by a doctor who suffers from insomnia.'

'I do not have insomnia.'

'Really?'

He frowned. 'Are you intent on questioning me because of something my sister told you?'

'Melody?' She seemed genuinely surprised with the question. 'Why would she tell me anything?'

'You said you spoke to her, spoke to other people at St Aloysius Hospital before I came to work here. What did they tell you?'

'They told me you were a brilliant surgeon.'

'They didn't tell you the rest of the gossip?'

'What are you talking about? What gossip?' she asked, clearly perplexed.

Ethan closed his eyes and slowly shook his head. His own paranoia had been his undoing. 'I'm sorry, CJ. I didn't mean to snap just now. 'I…uh…' He hesitated. 'Things happened to me and, uh…'

'I wasn't prying, Ethan, and I know what it's like to work in a big hospital where people love to gossip. Believe me, working in a small country town is just as bad.' She smiled, hoping it might settle him. 'I was just concerned that you weren't sleeping. That's all.'

'So you don't know why I'm here? Why I've taken the job as your locum?'

'Because you wanted a break from the rigours

of Sydney life. At least, that's what you wrote in the email you sent me with the application. However, given the conversation we've just had, I'm thinking there's more to it.'

Ethan toyed with his half-full cup on the table before wiping his sweaty palms on his robe. 'I… uh…' He paused and took a moment to concentrate on his breathing. 'I had a mild heart attack. It was just a warning,' he added quickly. 'I'm on a forced sabbatical from the hospital.'

'Oh, Ethan.' CJ shook her head sadly. 'I didn't know. Honestly. No one I spoke to said a word about that. They only told me how brilliant you were. No confidences were betrayed, just as I won't betray this one.' She placed one hand on her heart, her gaze filled with genuine concern. For a man who, only a few days ago, had told her he liked to keep his colleagues as colleagues and nothing more, she deeply appreciated him sharing such a personal piece of information about himself. 'Thank you for telling me. I appreciate your confidence.' They both took a sip of their teas, CJ mulling over everything he'd told her. 'So being here is supposed to be a change in pace for you?'

'Something like that.'

'I know you've only been here a few days, but how are you feeling so far?'

He breathed in deeply, filling his lungs. 'No tightness of chest.'

'You were having chest pains? For how long?' Her tone was inquisitive but professional, as though she was speaking to one of her patients.

'Professional concern?'

She shrugged one shoulder. 'I'm a doctor. I diagnose everyone—as do you. It's a habit.' When he didn't immediately answer her question, she prompted, 'How long have you been having these pains, Ethan?'

'Increasing in severity for the past six years.' His words were quiet yet matter-of-fact.

'Six years!' CJ gaped at him. 'What happened six years ago?'

'I moved to the city. I took up the position of Director of General Surgery. I began back-to-back research projects, which finally ended two months ago.'

'As well as heavy clinics, admin and operating lists?'

'Yes.'

'That's quite a workload.' CJ finished her tea and placed her cup on the table, her thoughts racing. 'No wonder your health has suffered but I'm also glad you're heeding the warnings, that you're not ignoring them.' She continued to think, voicing her thoughts out loud. 'So when you moved to the city, that was from the suburbs?'

'Yes.'

'From the house I described? The one with the nice furniture and big garage?'

'Yes.'

'You moved from that to a small city apartment?' Her brow was puckered in a frown as she tried to add two and two, but wasn't coming up with four as the answer. 'You said the commute was too much?'

'I'd taken up the directorship. I needed to put in longer hours.'

'But why take the directorship in the first place if you knew it would take you longer to comm—' She stopped, the frown disappearing, only to be replaced by a dawning realisation. 'You were in a relationship.'

'Yes. I was married.'

'The marriage ended, you moved from the suburbs, took up the directorship and lived a block away from the hospital. You threw yourself into your work, almost literally.'

'Yes.' Ethan stood and picked up both their cups, taking them to the sink.

'I understand marriage break-ups. Mine was no picnic and if Quinten hadn't passed away, we would most definitely be discussing our separation and divorce right now.'

He turned from the sink, shoving his hands into the pockets of his robe. 'My marriage didn't break up because my wife and I got divorced, CJ. My wife, Abigail—that was her name… Abigail…' He clenched his jaw and looked down at the floor before raising his gaze to meet hers. 'Abby died.'

Time seemed to stand still, the sound of the clock's second hand becoming duller as she stared at him with a mixture of compassion and pain. 'That's the reason I left the suburbs and threw myself into my work. To forget the pain, to forget the anguish, to just…forget.'

With that, he turned on his heel and headed to the door that led to his part of the house. A moment later, he was gone, only the sound of the ticking clock filling the silence as CJ sat there, absorbing everything he'd told her.

He was a widower who was still very much in love with the memory of his wife.

CHAPTER SIX

WHY THIS SHOULD matter so much, she wasn't sure. As CJ shuffled back to her room, brushing her teeth and emptying her bladder in the hope of getting a few decent hours of sleep, she thought back to those moments of awareness she'd experienced since Ethan Janeway had entered her life. Even tonight, holding his hand and feeling the strong, protective reassurance he exuded, had left a residual warmth deep down inside.

He'd stared at her yesterday, when they'd arrived at Whitecorn Hospital, as though he'd wanted to press his lips to hers. She'd been too busy reeling from the fact that she'd actually wanted him to follow through with that urge to even contemplate *why* he'd looked at her in such a way.

Why had he?' It made no sense. Was he simply looking for female companionship? If that was the case, why on earth would he consider a heavily pregnant woman? She was uncomfortable all the time and slept in a bed with a plethora of pillows. None of her sexy lingerie fitted her and probably wouldn't for some time, and soon she would be even more exhausted as the sole parent to a helpless baby. What on earth was attractive about any of that?

When Ethan woke the next morning, he was surprised he'd actually managed to sleep—again. 'This might actually become a habit,' he mumbled after he'd dressed for his first day on the job. Heading into the kitchen, he was pleased to have it to himself. While he ate breakfast, he kept glancing at the door through which CJ might walk through at any moment. Indeed, any little sound had him tensing with anticipation.

He still couldn't believe he'd not only told her about his heart attack but also about Abigail. Normally, he was a closed book—even with his family. It had taken Melody quite a while to get through to him and he knew his tenacious sister had only kept badgering him because she'd been incredibly worried about him…worries that had been proved correct.

He glanced once more towards CJ's door. Would she want to ask him more questions or would she respect his privacy? 'Probably the latter,' he murmured to himself. Both of them had been through marriages that, from what she'd said about her husband, hadn't been the happiest, and both of them had lost the opportunity to change the outcome. If Abigail had survived, he'd vowed to himself to be a better husband, to be more attentive, to help her, to listen to her more. Ethan sighed heavily. But she hadn't survived. She'd been taken from him and so had—

He stopped the thought. He may be trying to be more open, to be more communicative, especially with the people who mattered most in his life, but dwelling on such heartbreak would not help him at all this morning, especially when he had a clinic to attend to.

He glanced again at the door that led to her part of the house. Perhaps he should just check on her before he left; after all, with the anxiety she'd been exhibiting during their early morning *tête-à-tête*, he wanted to see for himself that she was indeed OK.

'Professional concern,' he muttered to himself as he knocked softly on the door. He'd check on her and then he'd be able to give Donna a report of what had happened, keeping CJ's doctor in the loop as to her patient's emotional state. He listened carefully for a moment but didn't hear anything. Slowly he opened the door and walked quietly towards her room.

The door was open and he heard her steady breathing before he saw her. Good. She was sleeping. Relaxed, sleeping and surrounded by a horde of pillows. He headed back to the kitchen relieved she was doing fine. After discovering his own wife had had pre-eclampsia and had kept it from him, Ethan was more than a little cautious when it came to pregnant women in their last trimester. As far as he was concerned, Abigail's death, and that of his gorgeous little baby girl, would not be in vain. Not on his watch.

CJ woke up in exactly the same position in which she'd gone to sleep, indicating she'd had a great sleep. Checking the clock, she was astonished to find it was after ten in the morning. Her first instinct was to scramble out of bed and rush over to the clinic, before she remembered that Ethan was here.

A smile instantly spread across her lips at the thought of her housemate. Ethan had come to Pridham so that she could rest and look after herself. Where she'd thought she might have been bored, right now, she felt a wave of stress leave her. That was very nice.

She sighed again and stroked her stomach. 'Thank you, sweetheart,' she told her baby, 'for letting Mummy have a good sleep. Do you feel good too, my honey?' Taking her time, CJ showered and dressed, singing in the shower and keeping up a steady dialogue with her unborn child. 'We're going to relax this morning because Ethan's doing the clinic. Then we'll go and visit some people this afternoon so we can introduce him to today's house call list.'

Secretly she hoped they could do the house calls in his awesome car. It was nice they shared the same interest, especially as she and Quinten hadn't really enjoyed the same hobbies or activities. Being able to talk to Ethan about car engines, about the stitching on the leather seats, about sourcing difficult parts that were out of stock—that sort of thing was wonderful. It meant she wasn't having to watch what she said in case she said something to upset him, as she had with Quinten.

Now, though, she realised the reason Quinten had often picked an argument with her had been because he'd felt guilty about wanting to leave her. They'd been a wrong fit right from the start. CJ sighed and headed to the kitchen. Once again the kitchen was tidy and she was thankful Ethan wasn't a messy slob, like Quinten.

Why she was comparing the two men, she had no idea. Perhaps it was because, apart from her father, they were the only other men she'd lived with. Yes, Ethan was showing promising signs of being a great housemate and, hopefully, a great friend, too. She ignored the little voice at the back of her mind that questioned the way that one smouldering look from Ethan could ignite a fire within her such as she'd never experienced before. She didn't want to acknowledge the fire or the spark because if she gave it too much thought, she might end up making another mistake, and where romance and love were concerned, she'd already made her fair share.

Besides, any crazy emotions she felt towards

Ethan were no doubt due to her overactive pregnancy hormones and nothing more. Once the baby was born, the crazy feelings would stop and she would return to normal…she hoped.

Added to that was the fact he'd told her about his wife. He was a widower who was still coming to terms with his grief. Perhaps being in Pridham would help him to heal, help him to accept his past and move forward into a less stressful future. CJ hoped she'd be able to support him through that, but as nothing more than a friend.

Her phone buzzed, bringing her thoughts back to the present, and she checked the text message. She was pleasantly surprised to find it was from Ethan, the message stating an ultrasound had been booked for her in two hours' time.

'How sweet. He's so sweet, baby,' she told her child. 'Sweet and thoughtful.' CJ shook her head. 'No. Not sweet, he's being professional and helpful…and thoughtful, but then he *is* a doctor and therefore is supposed to be thoughtful and helpful and professional.' She frowned as she decided what text message to send back but after typing several messages and then deleting them because they either sounded too personal or too sterile, she decided on sending emojis—one of a smiley face and one showing a thumbs-up.

'Why is this so hard? The line between housemate, friend, professional colleague, keeping out of each other's way or helping each other out, and…' She trailed off, sighing once more. 'Well, at any rate, I have time to get a few things done before the scan so up we get.' She rubbed the little foot that was sticking out, urging it back into place. 'Let's wash your new clothes so they're all ready when you arrive. That way, they'll feel all fresh and lovely rather than musty and starchy.' As she hadn't wanted to know the sex of the baby, CJ had stuck with buying pastels and cute outfits that would suit either gender. By the time she was due at the hospital, the outside washing line was filled with the tiny outfits being blown gently by the autumn breeze, and CJ's nesting instinct had been satisfied.

As she walked across the road, she couldn't help the slight spring in her step and knew it was because she would be seeing Ethan soon. She felt good, she felt happy and it was simply because he'd cared enough to suggest making this scan appointment so her mind would continue to be at ease, especially through the night when her fears usually raised their ugly heads.

Stopping at the clinic first, she was interested to see how Ethan had been coping. As she walked into the waiting room, she found Donna quietly discussing something with Tania, two patients still waiting.

'What are you doing here? I was about to go

over and meet you at the hospital,' Donna stated as soon as she saw CJ. 'I hope you've been resting.'

'I can't be resting every minute of the day, Donna,' she countered with a good-natured smile. 'I slept in until ten o'clock, had a leisurely breakfast and managed to get all the baby's clothes washed and on the line.' She paused for a moment. 'Wait—what do you mean, you were going to meet me at the hospital?'

'For the ultrasound,' Donna stated. 'Ethan asked me to make the appointment. He seemed quite concerned about you.' Donna fixed CJ with a worried look. 'You should have told me you had concerns. You know I'm there to support you for whatever you need.'

CJ shrugged. 'I guess with Quinten always saying I made mountains out of molehills, I sometimes feel as though I'm still overreacting— to anything and everything. Besides, the neurotic thoughts I have in the middle of the night often ease during the light of day. And I did try to call you but you were at Whitecorn.'

Donna frowned. 'I didn't know you'd called.'

'Night sister answered your phone.'

'Ah, yes. I'd left it at the nurses' station before treating Mr Bartlett.'

'Oh, no. Mr Bartlett? Is he—?'

Donna held up her hand to stop CJ's questions. 'He's stable.'

She sighed with relief. 'He was another good friend of my dad's. I hope he's able to pull through.'

'You and me both.'

The phone on Tania's desk buzzed and she quickly answered it. 'Yes. I'll tell her,' she replied, then nodded to her colleagues. 'The sonographer is ready for you.'

'Head on over, CJ. I won't be far behind you,' Donna said.

'OK. Thanks.' CJ started to head out the door that led to the hospital but as she did so, Ethan came out of his consulting room with a patient. The patient stopped, grinning brightly at the sight of CJ. Pleasantries were exchanged, the patient placed their hands on the baby bump and gave their prediction as to the gender before heading towards the waiting room. All the while, CJ was highly conscious of Ethan's presence.

He'd looked mildly startled to see her when he'd exited the consulting room and after nodding and smiling politely at her, he'd stepped back and not said a word. After the patient had left, CJ found she couldn't move, found that she wanted to stay where she was and just be near him, despite knowing what she now did about his wife. It was odd.

'How's everything going?' she asked.

'Very well. Everything is set up—the consulting room, the computer system—to work like a well-oiled machine and that's exactly what's been happening.'

'Good. Good.' A moment of uncomfortable silence passed.

'Er…' Ethan gestured towards the direction of the hospital. 'Heading over for the scan?'

'Yes. Yes…thanks for letting Donna know. Sometimes I think I'm being too over-dramatic and other times—'

He held up his hand to stop her. 'You're welcome.' Another moment of strained silence passed. 'Uh… I'd better go call my next patient in.'

'Sure.' She jerked her thumb towards the hospital. 'I'd better have that scan.'

He nodded again, then took a step towards her and said softly, 'Let me know the results.'

CJ held his gaze and there it was again…a zinging of awareness between them, as though there was something happening between them that neither of them had either asked for, or wanted.

'I…uh…had hoped to be there but I have…' He pointed towards the waiting room.

She shook her head and smiled at his words. How sweet of him. 'Oh, it's OK. Of course you're busy and if anyone's going to understand—'

'It's you,' he finished for her. And there it was again, the undercurrent of a conversation they weren't articulating. CJ licked her suddenly dry lips and Ethan's gaze dropped to follow the action with great interest. 'I, uh…checked in on you this morning to ensure you were OK but you were sleeping. Very soundly,' he added as an afterthought, that gorgeous smile of his appearing and creating havoc with her heart.

It took a moment for her to realise what he was saying, and her eyes widened in mortification. 'I was snoring!' She raised her hands to cover her face and was rewarded with a soft chuckle from Ethan. The sound washed over her and filled her with utter delight before she removed her hands and heaved a heavy sigh. 'Well, you've already heard me being ill so let's just add snoring to the list.'

'Were you sick this morning?'

'No. Actually, I wasn't.' It wasn't until he'd asked the question that she realised she hadn't even thought about it.

'Probably because you were able to sleep in and not rush around first thing in the morning.'

'More than likely.' She smiled at him once more. 'And it's all thanks to you.'

He held up his hands but his smile was still in place. 'Hey, I'm just here doing my job. I'm not a hero or a saint.'

'Are you still here?' Donna remarked as she walked towards the two of them. Ethan quickly stepped back, putting distance between himself and CJ.

'I was just checking to see how Ethan was coping,' CJ remarked.

'He's doing fine. Now come on, the sonographer is waiting for you.' Donna put her hand in the middle of CJ's back, urging her forward. 'Let Ethan get back to work. He still has several patients to see before house calls this afternoon.'

'I'll see you then,' CJ said to Ethan over her shoulder as Donna continued to usher her towards the hospital. Ethan knew he shouldn't stand there and watch her go but it was only a second later that she disappeared from view.

'What the heck just happened?' he whispered to himself as he headed to the waiting room to call his next patient through. As he worked his way through the rest of the clinic, he kept his questions at the back of his mind. Why was it that whenever he was within close proximity to CJ he couldn't stop staring at her mouth? He'd told her about his wife, how he was a widower, so clearly she understood that he was a man who hadn't dealt with his grief…didn't she? Perhaps he needed to make it clear that he wasn't interested in a relationship with anyone. He'd told her he wanted to just do his work and when his contract was up he planned to return to his life in Sydney.

But as he wrote up the notes for his last patient, he couldn't help but compare the life he'd had in that small apartment to the one he now enjoyed here. Although he'd only been in Pridham for less than a week, with the people he'd met, the acceptance he'd received, the support he'd been given, he had to admit he found it quite encompassing. He'd been able to breathe deeply, to fill his lungs completely and without stabbing pains. When he'd checked his own blood pressure, it was to find it at a far more acceptable reading and he was actually sleeping three to four hours per night. How could he be seeing such incredible results in such a short space of time?

Was it down to CJ's easygoing manner? He did like hearing the sound of her voice, he did like seeing her smile and, more importantly, he liked being the one to *make* her smile. He liked the way she smelled, of sunshine and happiness. He liked her gumption, that she accepted her lot in life and was prepared to get on with what needed doing. She wasn't wallowing in a pit of despair, lamenting about being left as a single parent. Naturally she had concerns and he was honoured that she'd felt comfortable enough to share them with him, and that he'd been able to do something to help.

He glanced at the clock on the wall. She should well and truly be done with her ultrasound by now and he wondered what the results were. Was she feeling more relaxed, more at ease? Was her blood pressure stable? Did she have any excess swelling around her ankles? He wanted to remain vigilant, to ensure she didn't fall victim to the same condition that had taken his wife. Granted, the circumstances were different and CJ was definitely looking after herself, but preeclampsia could turn to eclampsia far too quickly and then…

At the sound of feminine laughter, laughter that sounded a lot like CJ's tinkling laugh, coming from the direction of the waiting room, Ethan stopped his thoughts from progressing into the dark abyss, and quickly finished his work before heading out to where she was.

Sure enough, CJ was there, sitting in one of the waiting-room chairs, her feet up on a stack of magazines on the coffee table. Donna was leaning against the receptionist counter and Tania was twirling a pen between her fingers. His gaze settled back on CJ, pleased to see her resting.

'How did everything go?' He wasn't going to beat around the bush. She was his colleague and he was worried about her.

'Good.' She smiled brightly and rubbed her belly.

'Blood pressure is down, swelling is within normal parameters and the baby's head is engaged. I've also done a urine test—all clear, no protein.' Donna was the one to give him the medical report and he smiled at her before taking a closer look at CJ's ankles for himself. Yes, they were good. The tension started to leave him now that he knew she really was OK.

'Are you all right?' CJ asked him softly as the telephone rang. Tania answered it and told Donna it was for her. Donna headed off to her consulting room and Tania went to the bathroom. It wasn't until they were alone that she reiterated the question.

'Yes, I'm fine. It's you I've been concerned about.'

'You have?'

'Of course.' He sat down in the chair opposite her, the coffee table between them.

'Why?'

'Why? Because, as I'm sure you know, a lot of things can go wrong in the last trimester. It's better to be safe than sorry.'

CJ smiled. 'Are you always this adamant with the patients? Don't get me wrong,' she continued before he could respond, 'it's a good thing, especially in general practice.'

'Not all surgeons are scalpel happy,' he replied. 'Some of us actually do care about our patients.' Even as he said the words, he knew he hadn't been as concerned about some of his patients as he should have been. It was simply because he hadn't wanted to engage with the personal aspect, preferring to leave that up to his registrars. Getting personally involved with people would have required the wall he'd built around his heart to be broken down and he hadn't been ready for that. He wasn't sure if he was ready for it now but whether he wanted that wall to come down or not, it was happening and it was all because of the woman opposite him.

'Ready for house calls?' she asked, lifting her feet from the table and shifting in her chair, preparing to lever herself up. Ethan was quickly at her side, holding out his hands to help her up. 'Thank you.' As she stood, he once again found himself in close proximity to her hypnotic gaze and encompassing scent.

Neither of them moved; neither of them seemed to be breathing. The world around them had come to a standstill, as though they'd somehow been able to press the pause button in order to concentrate on exactly what was flowing between them.

'You smell really good.' Her words were barely audible and he couldn't help but stare at her perfectly shaped mouth, wondering if it would taste as good as it looked.

'So do you,' he returned.

'Stop looking at me like that.' CJ's gaze was flicking between his eyes and his mouth and he realised in that one split moment that whatever it was he was feeling towards her—something that had no name and no real substance—was reciprocated. She could feel it, too.

'I can't seem to help myself.'

'None of this makes any sense.' Again her words were so softly spoken it was as though they were communicating telepathically.

'I know.'

'But it's there. We're not imagining this?'

'If we are, then we're both sharing the same dream.'

'I want you to kiss me but if you do, I don't know what it will mean and that just confuses me further.'

There it was again, that complete and utter sense of open honesty that summed up CJ's entire personality. All her words did was to fan the fire deep within him, the fire that he hadn't even realised had been reignited, the fire of desire, of passion, of need. How was it possible for his world to have been tipped upside down so fast?

'I *want* to kiss you.' He kept his gaze trained on her mouth as he spoke, shaking his head slowly from side to side. 'I know it's wrong and stupid and impulsive and confusing but the desire is there. I don't know how or why…' He breathed slowly as he closed the small distance between them, drawn to her as though it was the most natural thing in the world. He was still holding her hands, still touching her, and whether it was that combined with the pheromones surrounding them that propelled him to within the close proximity of her mouth, there didn't seem to be any force there to stop him.

'This is lunacy,' she managed to whisper, right before his lips brushed a feather-light kiss to hers.

CHAPTER SEVEN

THE MOMENT SEEMED to last for an eternity, yet in reality it was no longer than a split second. Ethan pulled back, unable to compute the different thoughts surging through his mind. He'd just kissed another woman. That alone was enough to help him ease back, to stare into her half-closed eyes and resist the dreamy message she was silently sending him to repeat the action. He wanted to do it again, to continue to explore the sweet secrets her mouth offered, but the fact remained that he'd kissed a woman who wasn't Abigail and the realisation caused his gut to knot with guilt.

Dropping her hands as though burnt, he took a giant step back, almost tripping over the coffee table and knocking several magazines to the floor. To aid in covering his confusion and panic at what had just happened, he immediately bent down to retrieve the magazines, putting them back onto the table and taking another step away from her.

'I'll…uh…' He pointed towards the door. 'I'll go get the car ready.' With that, he gave her a wide berth before exiting through the front door. As he walked out, he heard Tania come back into the waiting room and realised how close they'd come to having their kiss witnessed.

What on earth had he been thinking? He hadn't. That was the answer. He hadn't been thinking. He'd allowed himself to get side-tracked, to relax, to let his guard down. 'This is what happens when you don't keep focused, when you listen to others and start to interact with the world.' Ethan continued to mutter to himself as he walked across the road to CJ's garage and unlocked the outer door.

His car. His beauty of a car. It had always been able to relax his stress. He glanced over to the workbench in the corner and saw a container of polishing cloths. Without further thought, he grabbed a cloth and began to rub it gently over the car's body, as though wiping away his turbulent thoughts and re-setting his mind to exhibit a more professional demeanour.

He was here to do a job. He was here to look after the patients until CJ's maternity leave finished. Where he'd been looking forward to spending time with her doing house calls this afternoon, he now longed for the time when he could do the house calls on his own. She would be at home, looking after her baby, and he would be either stuck in the consulting room or his bedroom, not daring to engage with her lest she should once again capture his attention with her dreamy green eyes and luscious smile.

'I'm sorry, Abigail,' he remarked as he threw the cloth back into the container and pulled the keys from his pocket. Yet as he slipped behind the wheel of the car, all he could think about was how much his wife had loathed the vehicle. She'd been angry about the time he'd spent with the car, calling herself a restoration widow. It had been an escape for him when their problems had become insurmountable. If he'd known how much she'd been suffering, would he have spent more time with her? And would it have made a difference?

He shook his head slowly as he buckled his seat belt and started the engine. He wondered if Abigail would be happy he'd kissed another woman, that he hadn't been able to stop thinking about another woman, that he was eager to spend time with another woman? He really hoped so. But she'd probably be annoyed that he still loved the car. He loved to polish it, to tinker with the engine and to feel his tension decrease as he went on long drives.

As he reversed the car to the front of the clinic, he saw CJ come out, a medical treatment bag in her hands. Leaving the engine idling, he quickly climbed from the car and took the bag from her, placing it securely on the small back seat. Then he held her door and helped her into the car, clenching his jaw and doing his best to ignore the powerful surge of awareness that spread from his hands and up his arms, before entering his bloodstream.

She thanked him for his help and once they were both buckled in, he waited for directions. CJ provided them whilst tying a scarf around her hair and slipping her sunglasses into place. After that, they drove along in silence and apart from the occasional 'Turn left at the next T-intersection,' and other navigational instructions, they both seemed quite content to absorb the serenity of the drive.

When they finally arrived at their first patient's house, Ethan stopped the car and turned the key to cut the ignition. The silence enveloped them but neither of them moved. CJ breathed deeply, then slipped off her scarf and sunglasses.

'It really is an incredible machine.' She stroked the dashboard. 'Thank you for the relaxing drive,' she told the car, then undid her seat belt and turned to look at Ethan. 'And thank you for doing the steering part.'

His smile was instant and she felt the earlier tension that had surrounded them begin to abate. He'd brushed a kiss to her lips. It wasn't as though he'd been making a pass at her but rather openly acknowledging that there were high levels of awareness pulsing between them. For CJ, that acknowledgement, that she wasn't the only one experiencing those sensations, was enough... for now. Her focus needed to be elsewhere, especially after today's ultrasound. The baby's head was engaged, and could be born at any point within the next week.

'Who's first on the list?' Ethan asked as he climbed from the car, quickly coming around to help her out.

'Thanks. I'm looking forward to the day when I can get in and out of a car without such a hassle.' He let go of her hand the instant she was standing and steady on her feet. Her smile faded and she glanced at him from beneath her lashes as he retrieved her bag. She needed to remain focused and professional so CJ cleared her throat and answered his question. 'Molly Leighton. She's almost sixty-two and she's been suffering badly from stress. She's been the manager of one of the larger vineyards for the past forty years. I keep suggesting she retire but she won't hear it. She's had high blood pressure, chest pain and a spate of mouth ulcers but—oh, you met her husband the other day. Toby—the cleaner. The one swinging the floor polisher at Whitecorn District.

He nodded. 'Manuka honey?'

'Correct. Molly needs to slow down and smell the roses but instead she works herself into a frenzy. She almost didn't speak to me again when I prescribed four weeks off work.' CJ shook her head. 'What that woman needs are some grandchildren to help her unwind but there's no chance of that on the horizon.'

'Let me guess. You're going to let her help you with yours.'

'And why not? I need help, Molly needs to slow down. It's a win-win situation.'

'And what about your child?'

'It wins as well because it will be smothered with love.' CJ shook her hair free in the wind, running her hands through the locks. He glanced across, instantly mesmerised by the way her hair was flowing gently in the breeze, the golden locks glinting in the sun, her long neck exposed in the autumn sunshine. Had she no idea how incredibly beautiful she was?

'Shall we go in?' Without waiting for him to answer, she walked up the front path and knocked on the door. It was flung open almost immediately by a woman dressed in a casual suit with her dark hair immaculate and her make-up perfect.

'Come in, CJ. Oh, and you've brought the new Dr Janeway, too. Toby told me about meeting you.' Molly ushered them both inside. 'Tea? Coffee? I've made some fresh scones.'

'That would be lovely,' CJ responded at the same time Ethan refused. 'Now, Ethan, you *must* try one of Molly's scones, especially when they're fresh from the oven. They are mouth-watering.'

She'd turned to face him as she spoke, so her back was to Molly. Her eyes conveyed an urgency that she wanted him to accept Molly's offer. He smiled at their patient. 'In that case, how could I possibly say no?'

Molly literally beamed. CJ hadn't seen her smile like that in a very long time. As Molly headed to the kitchen, Ethan spread his hands wide, as though silently asking why she'd made him accept. 'Cooking is the only thing that seems to be taking Molly's mind off the fact that she's not working. Besides, part of the reason for house calls is to provide a holistic approach to general practice medicine. Everywhere we go today, we'll be force-fed food and drink, which…' she rubbed her belly '…is good for the baby but bad for my bladder.' CJ chuckled at her own joke but as Molly came back into the room, carrying a tray of scones and drinks, she quickly stopped.

They sat in the 'good' lounge room on plastic-covered sofa chairs, CJ willing Molly to relax. Molly's recent tests had shown her mouth wasn't the only place where an ulcer might be brewing.

'Have all my test results come back?' Molly asked, getting straight to the point.

'Not yet but I'm fairly certain you do have an ulcer in your stomach.'

'Might the manuka honey help that, too?

After all, it's worked extremely well for my mouth ulcers.'

'Yes, so Toby was telling me. That's great news.'

'When can I go back to work? I've baked all the recipes in one book and am about to start on the next book. Toby's complaining he's starting to put on too much weight.'

'I'm sorry, Molly, but if you return to work too soon, it might cause more problems. The last thing we want is for the ulcer to perforate. First, we need to start treatment for the ulcer and I can't do that until the tests are confirmed.'

Molly crossed her arms and sighed huffily, clenching her jaw and shaking her head. Every muscle seemed to be clenched and CJ's concern for the other woman's blood pressure increased.

'CJ, you were right.' Ethan's deep voice broke through the tension of Molly's demeanour. 'These scones are incredible. Molly, you're a marvel in the kitchen.' He smiled at their patient and CJ watched as the other woman instantly relaxed, a slight blush colouring her cheeks. Did he have this effect on *all* women?

'Right. Let's take your blood pressure and have a look at your mouth and throat. I'll ring the path lab in Sydney to see how much longer those results will be.'

'I can do that,' Ethan offered. 'I have contacts at the lab and might be able to put a rush on the results.'

Molly looked at him as though he'd hung the moon and when CJ took Molly's blood pressure, she was pleasantly surprised at the lower BP rate. 'Good. Much, much better. Whatever you're doing is working.'

'Looks as though I'll be starting on savoury baking treats tomorrow,' Molly sighed.

'Well, if you ever find you have too many treats...' CJ rubbed her belly '...the baby's been quite famished of late so send them my way.'

Molly nodded. 'I'll make sure I do that.'

It wasn't much longer before they took their leave and once they were back in the car and CJ had given Ethan directions, she thanked him for his help.

'You were like a de-stressing machine for her. I think it's mainly thanks to you that we'll be getting delicious food from Molly.' She put her scarf and sunglasses back on but as the clouds above were starting to darken a little, Ethan decided to put the soft top up just in case.

'It's good to see you still have a healthy appetite,' he remarked. 'Many women don't eat that much during their last few weeks of pregnancy.'

CJ chuckled. 'No such luck with me. Baby is definitely hungry all the time.'

He smiled. 'Every pregnancy is different.' He turned the key in the ignition and the engine purred to life. 'Where to next?' CJ gave him directions to the next house call, which was a good fifteen-minute drive away. 'I don't mind,' he stated as he started the engine once more. This time, with the soft top up, it was easier for them to hear each other speak. 'Getting to drive around these roads with the incredible scenery is one perk of the job I'm definitely enjoying.'

'I'm pleased to hear it,' she responded, now curious to discover what he thought might be other perks of the job. Was kissing her one of them? She cleared her thoughts and focused on their next patient. 'This next case is concerning but also interesting. Margaret is thirty-two weeks pregnant and, from the tests I've run, I'm fairly sure the baby has foetal alcohol syndrome.'

'Really?' The tone in his voice instantly changed, and as he spoke, his words were clipped and direct. 'I've had some experience with this.'

'You have?' She was surprised. 'You've had a patient with foetal alcohol syndrome? Huh.'

'She wasn't a patient,' he remarked quickly. 'Do you have a copy of the test results here?'

CJ nodded. 'I've got all the files on the patients we're seeing today on my tablet computer.' She tried to reach into the back to the medical bag and eventually succeeded, pulling out the device and turning it on. As they drove along, she read out Margaret's most recent test results. 'Again, I'm waiting to hear back on the last round of tests, which will hopefully confirm my suspicions.'

'What's her background?'

'Margaret works at her parents' winery, and has been drinking wine since she was about thirteen. Not excessively back then, and always under her parents' control.'

'Do they drink?'

'Yes. Again, not excessively but constantly.'

'Clearly you think the baby's in danger?'

'I'm not sure. I only know what I've read in the information published and that's still not conclusive. If we could figure out a way to get Margaret to cut down the drinking, it would help. She says she's not drinking as much as before but I'm concerned.'

'Is she married?'

'Yes, but her parents and husband have insisted she quit work for the moment and concentrate on the baby. She had a lot of bleeding early on in the pregnancy,' CJ added by way of explanation. 'They didn't want her to miscarry but now I'm concerned that they've wrapped Margaret so tight in the proverbial cotton wool that the poor woman isn't able to do anything now.'

'Very over-protective?'

'Yes, and I think the solitude might be driving her crazy at the moment because of picking season. Both her husband and her parents are working longer hours than usual.

'I've been monitoring Margaret in between her visits to the obstetrician, and as you're helping with my list, that job will now fall to you, hence why it's important you meet her.'

'Have you raised your concerns with the obstetrician?'

'Of course, and between the two of us we're monitoring the situation closely. However, I would really value your opinion, too.' She pointed. 'Go left up here.'

He turned the car into a long, rambling driveway that was lined with trees. At the end of the driveway was a large, architecturally designed modern homestead, with all sorts of different angles here and there. 'Interesting.'

'It may look odd from out here but inside every room affords an exceptional view of the vineyard.'

'This is Margaret's house?' He brought the car to a halt in the curved gravel drive and quickly went around to help CJ out.

'Her *family's* house. Margaret and her husband live in the west wing of the house and her parents in the east wing.'

'Let's see what we're faced with,' he muttered, after he'd grabbed the medical bag and they'd headed up the curved steps to the front door, CJ hanging onto the handrail to assist her ascent.

'Dr Nicholls,' Margaret said with forced joviality upon opening the door. 'What an unpleasant surprise.'

CJ glanced briefly at Ethan and then back at

their patient. Margaret leaned heavily on the door
before letting go and staggering slightly away
from them. This wasn't good.

'Come to check up on me, no doubt. See that
I'm doing the right thing. You shouldn't have
worried. I have my husband, my parents, my
in-laws *all* checking up on me.' Margaret had
gone into the living room and sat down on the
leather lounge. There was half a glass of wine
on the small table in front of her. CJ sighed and
followed, opening the medical bag and taking
out the blood-pressure monitor.

'Let me take your blood pressure, Margaret.'

'If it'll make you happy,' she slurred, and held
out her arm. As CJ took her BP, Margaret glared
at Ethan. 'Brought a little friend with you.'

'This is my colleague, Dr Ethan Janeway. He'll
be filling in for me while I'm on maternity leave.'

'No doubt sticking his nose into everyone's
business, just like you. Giving advice where it's
not wanted. That's all you doctors are good for.'

'We're also here to help you,' CJ said.

'You sound like my mother.' Margaret cleared
her throat and mimicked in a nagging voice,
'Call the doctor if you have any pain. Just put
your feet up. That's our grandchild you need to
look after. Don't do anything.' She growled the
last. 'Just lie there all day, be a vegetable and
provide nourishment for the baby. Baby, baby,

baby. I wish Doug had never talked me into having this baby.'

'You don't mean that, Margaret. It's just the drink talking,' CJ soothed as she reported Margaret's BP to Ethan. Both of them shared a concerned look.

'It is not. I didn't want this child in the first place.'

'How much have you had?' It was the first time Ethan had spoken and Margaret glared at him.

'Don't you presume to come in here with your high and mighty ways. I don't have to answer any of your questions.'

'How much have you had?' Ethan's tone was firmer and more insistent than before.

'How dare you question me?' Margaret's voice was becoming shrill.

Ethan glanced around the room and then stalked off through a doorway.

'How dare you take such liberties? This isn't your house.' Margaret went to stand but it was too difficult. CJ put a hand on her shoulder but the other woman shrugged it off. Ethan stalked back in with two empty red wine bottles and one that had just been opened.

'Call the ambulance. I want her admitted.'

CJ pulled out her cellphone and made the call.

'Y-you can't do this. You can't just d-drag me off to hospital,' Margaret stammered.

'We can if we think either you or the baby is in danger,' Ethan told her.

'The baby. There it is again. Ruining my life.'

'You're doing an excellent job of ruining *its* life as well,' he replied firmly. 'CJ, pack her some clothes and call her husband.' He offered CJ his hand to help her to her feet.

'Leave Doug out of this. He has nothing to do with this.' Margaret was defiant as CJ left the room.

'He is the father of your child. He has a right to know where his wife and child are.'

'I'm staying right here. You can't make me go to hospital and the baby is fine. It kicked me all last night and the only time it really stops is when I have a glass of wine.' Her words had started out tough but ended on a sob.

Ethan could see the emotional anguish Margaret was in but knew he needed to keep the firm line if he was going to get through to her at all.

'It's ruined my life,' Margaret's slurring words continued. '*I* was important before I got pregnant. I helped my father, I ran the business, *I* was important and now…now I'm just an incubator. They won't let me do anything. They won't let me even look at the paperwork.' Tears started falling but Ethan still kept his distance.

He walked over to the hallway where CJ had disappeared and called to her. 'Margaret needs you,' he said when CJ returned. She walked into the room to find Margaret sitting on the lounge, rocking slightly backwards and forwards, her hands covering her face as the tears poured out. She rushed over and placed her arm about the other woman, reaching into her pocket for a clean tissue.

'Here.' Margaret took it, turning slightly in CJ's direction, and cried.

'*You* know how hard it is,' Margaret wailed.

'Yes, I do.'

'But at least you could keep on working. At least you haven't been told the only thing you're good for is providing for the baby. I can't even blow my nose without them worrying about the baby.'

'I know,' CJ soothed. 'They stopped worrying about you, didn't they?'

Margaret cried harder. The next time CJ looked up, Ethan had gone. She wasn't sure where but she didn't see him again until the ambulance arrived.

'Margaret.' CJ gently shook the other woman's shoulder. She'd cried herself dry before dozing off. 'Margaret. The ambulance is here.'

'Huh? Why do I need to go?'

'So we can check that you and the baby are all right. Your blood pressure is lower than it should be and you have some swelling around your ankles.'

'Is that bad?' Margaret now looked concerned.

'It's not good. Come on,' CJ urged. Thankfully, the fight seemed to have been knocked out of Margaret and she was a compliant patient during the transfer to Pridham District Hospital. Ethan and CJ drove behind the ambulance and once they'd arrived they settled Margaret into a room.

Ethan filled out the paperwork for the tests he wanted Margaret to have. 'We'll need to keep you in overnight, which is why Dr Nicholls packed a bag for you.'

'Yeah, yeah.' Margaret closed her eyes. 'Just go away and let me sleep.'

'Probably a good idea,' CJ said as they went out of the room. Margaret needed to sleep off the alcohol and here she could do it where they could also monitor her condition. 'I'll be around later tonight to check on her,' she told Bonnie, the CNC.

'No. *I'll* be around later tonight,' Ethan contradicted. 'CJ will be at home, resting.'

Bonnie nodded in agreement. 'Glad to see *someone* can make her rest. See you this evening, Dr Janeway.'

'Were there any other house calls for today or can they wait until tomorrow?' Ethan asked CJ.

CJ checked the list on her computer. 'None that are urgent. I'll have Tania put them onto Wednesday's house call list.'

'Good. What else do you need to do now?' he asked as he escorted her out of the hospital.

'Write up notes for the patients we've seen today and then email them to the surgery.'

'Right. You head back home, I'll do the paperwork and put my car in the garage.' He looked pointedly at CJ. 'Put your feet up and rest.'

'But I'm hungry. I was going to cook dinner and—'

'I'll cook dinner. If I get home and find you standing…' He let his words trail off and shook his head. There was something about his stance, the abruptness in his voice that made her concerned.

'Ethan, are you all right?'

'I just need you to rest, to put your feet up, to ensure that you and the baby are OK.' He clenched his jaw and CJ decided she'd simply do as he asked, especially as she was rather exhausted. As she headed across the road, leaving Ethan to do the work, CJ admitted that seeing Margaret behave in such a way had indeed been upsetting.

CJ's pregnancy hadn't been planned. In fact, when Quinten had told her he was leaving her, that he didn't love her, CJ had never thought they'd share one last night…one night when she'd foolishly thought she'd be able to change his mind, to show him that she was as adventurous in the bedroom as the next woman. Quinten hadn't seen it that way at all. Instead, after what she'd thought was a rekindling of their love, he'd kissed her forehead, told her she'd been great but that he couldn't stay here, living with her in this pokey little town where nothing ever happened.

Then, still lying in their bed, she'd watched him pull an already packed suitcase from the cupboard and head for the door. He'd had it packed even before they'd started to make love? In stunned disbelief, she'd put the question to him. 'Why did you even bother? If you'd already made up your mind to leave, why even bother?'

'Hey. I'm a red-blooded male and you were fantastic, sweetheart, but… I've had better.' He'd started out of the room.

'Wait.' CJ had grabbed her dressing gown and followed him as he'd walked to the front door. 'So this is it? We're done? Just like that?'

Quinten's answer had been to sigh tiredly. 'CJ, we've been over for years now. You know it. I know it.' He'd picked up his car keys, then turned to give her a once-over. 'Let's not pretend any more. You and I, we don't…fit.'

With that, he'd walked out the door, walked to his car and driven away, the tyres squealing on the bitumen road. She'd wanted to shout at him, to slam the door, to release the hurt and pain he'd inflicted on her with his horrible words, but that wasn't what she'd done.

Now, as she sat at the kitchen table, pickles,

chocolate spread and bananas in front of her, CJ spoke softly to her baby. 'I came inside, little one. I pulled the sheets off the bed and I washed them. I wanted to wash every aspect of him out of my life that night.'

'Who...are you talking about?' Ethan's deep voice sounded behind her and it was only then that CJ realised she'd been sitting at the table for quite some time. He walked into the kitchen, smiling softly when he saw the food in front of her, and sat down nearby. 'Is everything all right?'

CJ sighed slowly. 'I was just thinking about how Margaret's pregnancy was planned, and look how it's turned out. Yet my pregnancy wasn't planned, and I just can't wait for this baby to come and complete my life.' She picked up a chocolate-smothered pickle and chewed thoughtfully. 'It's sad how things work out, never as you thought they might. I really hope Margaret is able to stop drinking, to see that the baby isn't her enemy. It just so sad,' she repeated.

Ethan was quiet for a moment before picking up one of the slices of banana and eating it. CJ was more than happy to share her food with him and a small thread of happiness made its way through her melancholy aura. 'Were you talking about your husband?'

She nodded. 'I was thinking about the night he left. I thought we were reconciling, that we were going to be able to fix the problems he'd already raised, but that wasn't the case. Instead, he used me and discarded me. I just needed to wash him out of my life, to pack up everything he'd left behind that reminded me of him and get rid of it, but after washing the sheets, exhaustion set in. I slept that night in my dad's room, the room that's now yours, wrapped up in blankets and curled into a tight little ball, feeling so small and so little.'

'You didn't pack everything away?'

'Four hours after Quinten drove off, the police knocked on my door to tell me he'd been killed. He'd driven from here, picked up the woman he'd been having an affair with, who lived in Whitecorn, and then taken a turn too fast on the road and ploughed his car into a tree, killing them both outright. After that, I felt… I don't know what I felt, except numb. Packing his things away felt too much like erasing him from existence and… I thought I owed him… I don't know… I owed him *something* but…' CJ shook her head.

Ethan reached over and took her hand in his. 'You owe him nothing.'

'Don't I owe the baby at least some memory of who their father was? Sure, Quinten didn't know about the baby—neither did I—but—'

'All you owe this baby is love and you're already providing that. You're looking after yourself, you're asking for help, you're eating strange foods but you're resting.' He smiled as he spoke. 'You're doing all the right things and that's what counts.'

CJ looked at their hands, their fingers seeming to intertwine so naturally. His touch made her feel wonderful, reassured, confident about the tasks that awaited her. Still, she noted the sadness behind his eyes, a sadness that shielded repressed pain.

'Ethan,' she began softly, 'when your wife died…' At her words she felt his hand go limp and he tried to pull back but she held on for a moment longer. 'How did she die?'

He jerked his hand back and this time she let go. 'Why do you ask?'

CJ shrugged one shoulder. 'You mentioned you'd had experience with foetal alcohol syndrome and that it wasn't via a patient. Then, when you were talking to Margaret, I just had a…feeling. You just seemed overly concerned for her—which is good, I want you to be overly concerned with the patients—but I just sensed there might be more to it than you're letting on. And with me,' she continued, before he could get a word in edgeways, 'you're very concerned about me, that I don't overdo things, that I take it easy, that I rest and relax and do what's right for the baby. I don't mind. Everyone else in the district fusses over me and the baby but with you it seems…deeper. As though you're almost desperate to ensure both the baby and I are OK.'

'I thought that was the role of the GP, to ensure their patients have the right treatment.'

'I'm not your patient,' she pointed out.

'No. You're my new friend, and as I've been a confirmed workaholic for years and rarely have the time to *make* new friends, is it any wonder I'm concerned about your health?' He stood and walked to the kitchen bench, his back to her for a long moment before he turned to face her, his arms crossed, his expression closed.

'You're avoiding answering the question, Ethan, and I think I might have guessed why. I think I know how your wife died and I think it was due to complications with a pregnancy. That's why you're so worried about *me*. You're determined to make sure the same thing doesn't happen to me.'

As CJ spoke the words, she watched the blood drain from Ethan's face, and she knew she was right.

CHAPTER EIGHT

'YOUR WIFE DIED in childbirth?' She went to stand but he quickly held up a hand to stop her.

'You need to rest. You need to be off your feet. You need to ensure you don't…' He stopped, closing his eyes before saying with choked emotion, 'That you don't get pre-eclampsia.'

'Oh, Ethan.' CJ didn't care whether she was on her feet or not, she wanted to be near him, to comfort him, to be there for him as he'd been there for her the whole time he'd been in town, but he clearly didn't want that comfort, not at the moment. 'What happened?'

Ethan leaned against the bench, needing to keep the distance between them. He shouldn't be surprised that she'd figured it out. CJ Nicholls was a smart woman. However, the only reason she'd been able to figure it out was because he'd let down his guard—something he'd sworn to himself he would never do. He hadn't planned to let anyone inside the wall he'd built around his heart and somehow, without him fully realising it, mortar had broken down and bricks had crumbled, releasing light into the cavern…a light in the guise of the woman before him.

He knew she was waiting for him to speak but

first he had to deal with that nagging voice from deep within, telling him to just walk out the door, to leave, to snub her. The more he looked at her, seeing the genuine concern in her eyes, hearing the compassion in her tone, he knew if he was ever going to open up to anyone about his past, it would be this woman. She'd been through so much herself, she'd been honest with him from the very beginning and he instinctively knew that whatever he told her, it would be held in the strictest confidence.

'Abigail was always so organised, so in control. I was working day and night at the hospital and she resented that. At some point we stopped talking and I couldn't get through to her, so when I wasn't at the hospital, I was out in the garage with the car.' He shook his head sadly. 'She'd always tell me off for spending more time with the car than with her but…' He swallowed and chose his words carefully. There was no point in hiding from the truth any longer. 'Restoring the car relaxed me. She didn't.' Ethan spread his arms wide, then let them fall back to his sides. 'I was a bad husband. A bad father to my unborn child.'

'I doubt you neglected her completely, Ethan.' CJ's tone was reassuring.

'Of course not. I loved her. I loved the thought of her having our child, our little girl. I couldn't wait to be a dad, to have a family. That's why I wanted to get the car all done and sorted out so that when the baby came, I would have more free time to spend with both of them.'

'Tell me more about Abigail.'

His smile was natural. 'Abigail, as I said, was very self-sufficient, very directed. When we met at university, we became friends for a few years and then…things progressed into more than friends. Abby went into organisation mode. She had everything planned. How long it would take for us to save up and get our first house, where we should get married, when we would start having children. It was all in her clearly thought-out plan—sometimes even with colour-coded charts.'

CJ grinned at that. 'I admire people like that but that's probably because I'm so disorganised… Or, as my father used to term it, "creatively chaotic".'

Ethan walked over and pulled out a chair, sitting down and sighing. 'And that was my major mistake with Abby. I let her organise, I was happy to be organised. I thought that if she had worries or concerns, especially about the pregnancy, that she would tell me but she didn't. When she was getting angry with me for always being in the garage when I wasn't at the hospital, *that* was her cry for help. She didn't come out and say directly, *I'm scared, I'm worried, I don't feel well.* Instead, she just read book after book, scouring the internet, looking up different symptoms and trying to figure things out herself.'

'She wasn't a doctor?'

Ethan shook his head. 'No. Abigail did one year of nursing at university and changed majors to accounting.'

'That's a big change.'

'She was an academic at heart. Did her honours, her master's degree and finished her doctorate during the pregnancy. I was so proud of her. Order. Structure. Purpose.'

'You clearly loved her very much.'

'I did. I do. I always will.' Ethan tilted his head back and closed his eyes. 'But she's not here. She had swelling at the ankles, her blood pressure was up. She didn't want to worry me. That's what she said to me when we were in the ambulance, heading to the hospital. "I didn't want to worry you as I know you've been hectic at work." I felt so guilty. I still do.' He dragged in a deep breath, then opened his eyes and looked at CJ. 'Why didn't she tell me? I could have helped her. Why was she so scared that she couldn't tell me?'

'Ethan, you can't blame yourself. Even in today's world, with all the medical advancements we've made, things still go wrong.' CJ reached out her hand to him but he didn't take it. Couldn't. There was still something he had to tell her, something he hadn't told anyone, something only he and the staff in the room at the hospital where his baby girl had been born knew. He clenched his jaw and sniffed as he felt tears begin to threaten. Not only were they tears of grief but also tears of anger.

'Babies sometimes don't make it through childbirth, especially with something like eclampsia,' CJ continued.

'And birth defects.' The words were out before he could stop them and he sniffed once more.

'What?' The word was barely audible and she sat back up, her hand sliding from the table to rest protectively on her own child.

'My little girl…' No sooner were the words out of his mouth than the tears started to trickle down his cheeks. 'Ellie—my little Ellie—she was…she had…' He pursed his lips and accepted the clean tissue CJ fished from the pocket of her dressing gown. He dabbed at his eyes, then blew his nose.

'Abigail had been drinking. I'd had no idea. None whatsoever. She'd been so stressed from her studies, with the pregnancy, with me not being there, and she couldn't tell me any of that. She hid it all from me and then, when it was too late, when the eclampsia had taken hold, there was nothing to do but try and save the baby, but even then it was too late.' Another tear ran down his cheek and before he knew it, CJ had somehow shifted her chair around so she was closer to him. She put her arms around him and he let her. She held him close and he let her.

'Ellie lived for almost twenty-two hours. I changed her nappy, I held her, I told her… I… I loved her.' The grief, the pain, the despair of losing his daughter came to the fore and he cried like he'd never cried before. CJ did nothing but hold him, support him. She didn't ask questions. Instead, she cried along with him, sharing in his loss.

Eventually, he was able to ease back, looking around for more tissues. He spied the box on the kitchen bench and eased himself from CJ's arms, before bringing the box back to the table and sitting down again. His legs weren't strong enough to support him; every muscle in his body ached yet the relief at having finally told someone else about Abigail's deception and the resulting consequences was overwhelming.

'I gave Ellie a bottle and she wrapped her tiny fingers around one of mine.' He blew his nose again and exhaled a calming breath. 'I took photos of her but I've never shown them to anyone, I've never looked at them again.'

'I'm so glad you took some pictures of her. She deserves that, she deserves to be remembered and loved by you for ever.' As CJ spoke, a fresh bout of tears flowed down her own cheeks. 'You're an amazing man, Ethan, and you would have made an amazing dad.'

'How could you possibly know that?'

'Because of the way you talk about Ellie.' She gave him a watery smile. 'You use the same tone my father used to use when he was talking about how much he loved me and my sister, and my dad was a great dad.'

He absorbed her words for a moment, then asked again, 'Do you really think I would have been a good daddy?'

Her smile was bright and she nodded. 'I know it. The way you look after me, the way you make me rest—it all makes sense now.' It also explained the veiled anger and desperation she'd seen him convey towards Margaret. 'I'm not going to do anything to jeopardise the health of this baby or myself. That's why I brought you in, why I eventually agreed to hire a locum.'

'I know.' He reached out and brushed a few strands of hair from her eyes, tucking them behind her ear. 'You're willing to ask for help. You're open and honest about your limitations. I like that about you.' Whereas Abigail had hidden everything from him. She'd been drinking for months—he'd never known why—and whilst he carried his fair share of the blame in the situation, he'd also come to realise that Abby also bore that blame and had paid for it with her life.

Now, with CJ, it was as though a new world was being opened for him. A world with laughter and a tinge of hope on the horizon. Was it possible he didn't have to keep punishing himself by working day and night, staring down the barrel of an early grave? He stared into CJ's dazzling green eyes and cupped her cheek with his hand before leaning a little closer, the atmosphere between them changing from one of support to one of heightened awareness.

He couldn't stop looking at her mouth and she couldn't stop looking at his. It was as though leaning forward, bringing herself closer to him, to within kissing distance, was the most natural thing in the world.

'CJ.' He whispered her name, the sound soft, delicate and intimate. As he neared, their breath began to mingle, the pheromones blending to form a heady combination. When she licked her lips in anticipation, he exhaled slowly but continued to decrease the space between his mouth and hers.

Before she knew it, Ethan's lips were pressed to hers, much the same as they'd been before, but this time there was more pressure, with the heightened need to figure out exactly what existed between them. She breathed in a deep, shaky breath before sighing into the kiss.

Bringing his other hand up to fully cup her face, he took his time exploring the tastes and flavours she exuded. She was sweeter than anything he'd ever experienced. She filled his senses completely. He could feel himself going under, wanting more, needing more, and she didn't disappoint.

He'd thought that one kiss might get her out of his system. That one kiss might help him to sleep at night. That one kiss would be all he would ever need from her. He was wrong. Groaning, he leaned closer, sifting his fingers through her loose hair, the silkiness of the tendrils only adding fuel to the fire that was already burning wildly through him.

How was it possible to barely know someone yet feel such an undeniable attraction? How was it possible to trust someone, to experience the primal need to take everything being offered? And it was being offered, on both sides. Both of them were one hundred percent involved in the moment, in the heat and delight. What it meant, CJ had no clue but while the exquisite torture continued, she was going to ensure she savoured every moment.

This was passion as she'd never felt it before. How could he stir such incredible longing with a few teasing and exploratory kisses? It was incredible and she felt as though she were floating…lifted up on the wings of desire—desire she was thrilled to discover was mutual.

As though he wanted to continue the slow discovery of every part of her mouth and the secrets contained therein, he sighed with delight, his mouth moving over hers in a sensual caress—a

lover's caress. She wasn't sure how she was supposed to cope. She had thought she was on fire
before with his testing kisses but now…now the
flame had been fanned into something more—a
fire that was taking her senses up on an internal
climb so high, she felt as though she'd erupt like
bright fireworks. Fire-stars, she'd called them as
a child and now the term seemed appropriate to
describe how he was making her feel. Fire-stars
bursting brightly, one after the other as his mouth
moved carefully and meticulously over hers.

It was as though he had to memorise every
part of her. You do, he told himself, because this
moment in time needs to last you for ever. Now
that he'd done it, now that he'd given in to the
urge to kiss her, he wanted it to be thorough.

The way she responded, not holding back a
thing, had him losing his head completely. It was
just like her to be so honest with her emotions
and he had a glimpse of the love and promises
she would have offered to her husband. The man
had hurt her, broken her, used her and discarded
her. At that thought, Ethan's hands slipped from
her hair to her shoulders, somehow wanting to
convey the information that he wasn't that sort
of man, that he wasn't callous and calculating.
If she'd offered him such a gift, he would do everything in his power to cherish it.

That thought was enough to break the hold
the delightful taste of her had evoked upon his

senses. He broke his mouth free and pressed
kisses to her face. He shifted his chair, bringing it closer to hers before nuzzling her earlobe.
Was that what she was offering? Was she offering herself to him? He wasn't sure. He didn't
have a clear read on the situation. All he knew
was that her hair was soft and silky to his touch
as he brushed it out of the way so he could rain
kisses on the sensitive hollow of her neck.

'Mmm…' she moaned, and shivered slightly as
goose-bumps broke out over her skin. It was torture, sheer, sweet, torture, and she never wanted
it to stop. With an impatience she couldn't control she willed his lips to stop the pleasurable
torment and return to her mouth. 'Kiss me,'
she whispered, the words hardly audible, but he
heard them.

Her words made him smile and helped those
unwanted questions to be pushed to the back
of his mind once more. It had been far too long
since he'd felt this sort of desire, this sort of need,
this sort of promise. Whatever this was, she was
in it with him, side by side, clearly enjoying the
ride as much as he. He pressed another round of
kisses to the other side of her neck, enjoying the
way she moaned and shivered beneath his touch.
Finally, when he couldn't stand it any longer either, he brought his mouth back to hers.

They both relaxed into the kiss, their lips eager
to become reacquainted, eager to continue with

the journey into the unknown, unexplored desire that had been building between them since that first day in the supermarket. Even though it was all still new, he felt as though he'd been kissing her mouth for ever. The taste of her was genuine and her scent was a powerful, natural aphrodisiac.

Never had he expected such a gamut of emotions when he'd given in to the urge to kiss her. Her tongue lightly outlined his lips and he heard himself groan, amazed again at how this woman could override all his warning signals, his brick walls, and shoot him straight through the heart.

The heart?

The thought was enough to make him pull back. He cupped her face in his hands and stared down into her eyes, both of them breathing heavily. Her green eyes were glazed with pent-up frustrations and desire. Her lips were slightly swollen and pink—irresistible. Just gazing at her now had him wanting her all over again.

He wanted to give in but knew if he did, there was no way he'd have the willpower to stop things from taking their natural course. They kept gazing at each other as their heart rates gradually returned to normal. Her eyelids started to close and she rested her head on his shoulder, sighing contentedly.

'Sleepy,' she murmured, and couldn't help the yawn that escaped. She stayed where she was for a while, Ethan feeling her head become more heavier than usual. Eventually, he eased back, once more cupping her face in his hands as he looked down into her exhausted face.

'Go to sleep,' he murmured, and couldn't resist kissing the tip of her nose. He'd wanted to kiss her mouth again, to press promises to her luscious and addictive lips, but thought better of it. Losing control once was something he could live with. Repeating the action again and again would just be asking for trouble.

'Mmm…' Her eyes remained closed and she smiled at his words. 'I'll just clean up and—'

'Go to bed, CJ. I'll take care of things.'

'You always do that. You always say you'll take care of things.' As she spoke, she opened her eyes and looked at him. 'But you also need to take care of yourself.' Raising a tired hand to his face, she caressed his cheek. 'You've locked yourself away for so long, you've been filled with so many different emotions—anger, pain, disappointment.' CJ yawned again. 'Be kind to yourself, too.' Then she put her hands on the table in order to lever herself from the chair. Ethan quickly stood and helped her up.

'Sleep. I'll make some food and leave it in the fridge for you, ready for your early morning snack.'

'You don't have to—' She broke off as another yawn claimed her.

'Go lie down.'

'All right, Dr Bossy, I'm going.'

He heard her chuckle as she shuffled from the room and disappeared down to her end of the house. He sat there, listening to the sounds as she went to the bathroom before getting into her bed. How could his hearing be so acute, so in tune with every move she made? More to the point, how could he have given in to the urges he'd been doing his best to resist ever since he'd entered CJ Nicholls's world? He'd kissed her! He'd kissed his colleague…his *pregnant* colleague. What had he been thinking?

He hadn't.

Plain and simple—he hadn't.

The strange thing was, he expected to feel a world of guilt descend upon him again because he'd been unfaithful to Abigail's memory, but it didn't. If there was one thing kissing CJ had helped him to realise, it was that he had a right to be angry with Abigail. He hadn't wanted to before. He hadn't wanted to tarnish her memory, not when he'd been grieving the loss of both her and Ellie. His sister and brother had stood by him, his parents, too. They'd done everything they could to support him, none of them realising why he'd just shut everything out, why he'd moved into the apartment and why he'd never wanted to talk about it.

Lo and behold, six years later it was a caring

she spent in hospital made her realise that her situation is extremely serious.' CJ shook her head.

'Should Margaret and Doug get counselling? Should we hospitalise Margaret for the duration of her pregnancy?'

'I've tried the counselling route at the moment as Margaret does seem to like being at home but given she still has about another six weeks to go, perhaps we should consider hospitalisation.'

'What does Ethan think of the situation?'

Margaret was the one patient they'd discussed yesterday when CJ had been in the lounge room with her feet up when he'd arrived home from clinic. 'He said it doesn't look good. Margaret may still miscarry at any stage.'

Donna sighed. 'Has Ethan seen this type of thing before? Foetal Alcohol Syndrome?'

CJ thought back to what he'd confessed about his wife. 'He has, as a matter of fact, and because of that, he's done a lot of research into it.'

'Good.'

'The main problem Margaret faces is that if she doesn't stop drinking now, the likelihood that the baby will be born with some sort of deformity will increase. I've been reading up on it, too, but even now it might be too late and the baby might not even survive.'

'Does Margaret know this?'

'I've told her the facts. Ethan's told her the facts. I know the social worker came and saw her when she was in hospital and talked to her about the possibility of birth defects. We're doing all we can and we're not trying to scare her but rather inform her.' CJ sighed with exasperation. 'In the end, though—'

'It's up to Margaret.'

'Exactly.'

'I'll get Ethan to discuss the idea of prolonged hospitalisation with Margaret's obstetrician.'

'OK.'

'Or…you could tell him.'

'Me? Ask Ethan to talk to Margaret's obstetrician?'

'Yes. You live in the same house as him. It's not like you don't talk at all.'

CJ shook her head quickly. 'No. No. It's much better coming from you.'

Donna eyed her carefully. 'Does Ethan know you've seen Margaret?'

'Ethan isn't the boss of me,' CJ stated, lifting her chin a little.

'He told me he's been insisting you rest.'

'Insisting is a mild word. He won't let me do anything! Just because—' CJ stopped. Although she wanted to tell Donna what Ethan had shared with her, had told her about his wife and his unborn child, she didn't want to break his confidence. 'Because I'm pregnant, he thinks I'm useless.'

'You sound very indignant about it.' Donna

was looking at her as though she was sure CJ was hiding something. 'Yet when I tell you to rest, you don't sound nearly so put out.' A smile started to form on Donna's lips. 'I think you're a little bit attracted to our new locum. At least, that's the sense I got last week when you were standing in the waiting room about to kiss him!'

CJ gasped. 'You saw us!'

'It was purely by accident. I came out of my consulting room to check something with Tania but saw the two of you and quickly retreated.' Donna shifted forward in her seat. 'So? What was it like?'

CJ thought back to that day and slowly shook her head. 'It wasn't really a *kiss* per se.' Not compared to the ones they'd shared later on. 'More like a moment when we brushed lips.'

'A moment?'

'Half a moment. It was very brief, very light, very…' CJ trailed off, sighing softly before adding, 'Very nice.'

'So you *are* avoiding him. That's why you're out most nights. Visiting me, visiting Tania, visiting a plethora of other people.'

'What? Do you hold regular meetings to discuss my whereabouts?'

Donna laughed. 'Are you avoiding Ethan because of the way he makes you feel?'

CJ straightened her back and flicked her pigtails over her shoulder, determined to deny her friend's words, but the instant she opened her mouth, she slouched and covered her face with her hands. It was no use. 'He's so nice and wonderful and caring, as well as frustrating, infuriating and…sexy.' She dropped her hands. 'I like the way he smells. I like the way he walks. I like the way he talks. I really like him and that scares the living daylights out of me.'

'What's the problem?'

'Problem? Where do I start?' She spread her hands wide. 'How about the fact that his life is in Sydney and mine is here? How about the fact that I've already been burned by one man, that I'm not about to throw myself back into the fire. And the last reason why it just wouldn't work.' She pointed to her belly. 'I'm about to have a baby! All my time and attention and care is about to be completely focused on figuring out how to be a parent.' With her emotions in overdrive, while she'd been talking, tears had sprung to her eyes and she reached for a tissue and blew her nose. A moment later she closed her eyes and said softly, 'Here I am, on the brink of having Quinten's baby, and all I can think about is Ethan Janeway. I mean, what man in his right mind would be attracted to me? Look at me! I'm huge!'

'You're pregnant and you're all baby. You've watched your weight carefully and have hardly put any extra on, even with all your late night pickle and chocolate spread snacking.'

CJ gasped. 'He told you about that!'

'It's hardly a secret, CJ, but it wasn't Ethan, it was Idris at the grocery store.'

'Oh.'

'Once the baby's born, it won't take you long to get your figure back. You'll be your normal size again and everything will feel better.'

CJ dabbed at her eyes before blowing her nose. 'I know. It's all silly, it's all emotional but...' She sighed. 'It was *so* nice to think that he might be attracted to me, especially when I'm huge like this. Do you have any idea what that did for my self-esteem?'

'I can imagine. What's your plan, then? To go out visiting people at night until the baby's born?'

'Sounds good to me.'

'Does Ethan know where you are?'

She shook her head. 'I don't think so but I don't answer to him.'

'That doesn't sound like you.'

'Quinten needed to know where I was at all times and I often thought that was so sweet, that he was interested in me, and yet the truth of the matter was that he only wanted to know where I was so I wouldn't catch him having one of his many affairs.'

'Ethan isn't Quinten,' Donna pointed out softly.

CJ huffed and shrugged. 'I know but I still don't need to tell him where I am at every moment of the day. I don't ask where he goes. He gets up early and is out of the house before I've woken up, so I've taken to visiting people in the evening to give him some time to work, instead of hibernating in my bedroom.'

'That's very considerate of you.'

'If I didn't, then he'd probably go out and he's got nowhere to go.'

'True. Or here's a thought—you could just try talking to him.'

'I do talk to him but there's only so much we can say about our patients.'

Donna chuckled. 'Listen, once the baby is born, you'll feel better. Your life will settle down into a nice, easy rhythm and Ethan Janeway will return to Sydney and all will be forgotten.'

'It could be my hormones that are telling me I'm attracted to him when I'm really not.' She closed her eyes and shook her head. 'Man, that sounds silly when I say it out loud.'

'But why don't we blame those troublesome hormones at the moment?'

'Yes. Yes, I think you're right.'

'And after all he's the only good-looking, single man of your age in the vicinity.'

'True. Very true.'

'So there you go. Opportunity and motive, all of which you had absolutely no control over. You are not to blame.'

'Excellent.' CJ shifted out of the chair and stood. 'Thanks, Donna. I'm glad I came over tonight.'

'So am I. Go home, have a snack, get a wheat bag warmed up and lie down with a good book.'

'Sounds like the perfect prescription.' CJ hugged her friend, then said, 'I might just use your bathroom first. Junior's jumping on my bladder again.'

Ethan stared out the window at the dark and empty street. There weren't as many streetlights here as there were surrounding his apartment in Sydney. The night sky seemed darker, the stars seemed brighter, and he could swear there were more stars here than there were in Sydney.

Where was she?

'Ethan? Are you still there?'

'Yeah. Sorry, Melody. What were you saying?'

'That things are crazy at work. The director's resigned.'

'Oh, yeah. So who's going to take over being Director of Orthopaedics?' He turned away from the window and began to pace around the lounge room, returning a moment later to look out the window again when he thought he'd heard a noise. He'd spoken to his sister more in this past week than he had in the past year, finally managing to tell her the truth about Abigail and Ellie.

After they'd discussed things for a while, Melody had asked, 'Why are you able to talk about it now? Not that I'm complaining, it's just...you know, six years, Ethan, and *now* you can dis-

cuss things? You've changed—for the better—
and I think it all has to do with the different
pace of life in Pridham. You've been forced to
re-evaluate your life, to slow down, to breathe,
to—'

Ethan had cut her off, not wanting to discuss
every aspect of his life with his sister. However,
since then, Melody had taken to calling him,
wanting to chat, wanting to share things in her
life with him, and he was pleased she'd taken the
initiative. It made him realise just how far he'd
distanced himself from his family but, thankfully, they hadn't let him disappear completely.
He owed them for that, and he owed CJ for helping him to realise all this.

It was crazy how his housemate had come to
mean so much to him so quickly. He'd never
thought, when he'd made the decision to come
to Pridham, that this sort of thing would happen,
that he'd be able to open up and talk about his
pain with those who cared about him. He also
hadn't expected to be attracted to his new colleague and end up being desperate to kiss her.
Yet that's exactly what he'd done. It was ridiculous, though, because his life wasn't here in Pridham. His life was in Sydney, with his patients,
his surgery, his department. He liked working
in Sydney, he liked operating and was missing
it here in Pridham. Granted, the pace of life here

was much slower and, as far as his health went, it was doing him the world of good.

Except for this past week. Ever since he'd kissed CJ, he hadn't managed to get any proper sleep. It was little wonder, especially as his thoughts had been constantly churning about what the kisses might mean.

Why did they need to mean anything? That had been his main argument. Perhaps those kisses had just been a means of him releasing the anguish he'd kept locked away for so many years, a way of thanking CJ for helping him to realise he still had a lot to offer the world. However, it was his desire to press his mouth to hers every other time he'd seen her that was starting to do his head in. Where he'd thought the attraction for her would begin to wane, it had, instead, intensified. He'd wanted to kiss her even more, to further explore the sensations only she'd been able to evoke, which was the reason why he'd woken up very early the morning after those exquisite kisses and ensured he had been out of the house before she'd got up.

Since then, he'd done his best to give her a wide berth, not wanting to become a complication in her life. She had enough to contend with and although both districts of Pridham and Whitecorn were watching over her, pledging their support once the baby was born, the desire to gather her into his arms and keep her safe, to protect both CJ and her unborn child, was something Ethan was constantly fighting. *He* wanted to protect her. *He* wanted to keep her and the baby safe. But *why*? Was he merely trying to appease his subconscious? To save CJ and her child, when he'd been unable to save Abigail and Ellie?

Upon hearing another sound from outside, he went to the front door, opening it, but it wasn't her. He checked that the sensor lights were working so that whenever she finally did come home, she wouldn't be navigating her way to the door in the dark.

'Are you listening to me at all?' Melody asked again.

'I am. You're telling me the shortlist for the director of orthopaedics.' Ethan went back inside. 'Hey, isn't your department supposed to be getting a visiting professor or something like that soon?'

'In another few months. Hopefully, the new director will be installed by the time that happens.'

'You could do it.'

'Me? Be the director of orthopaedics?' Melody laughed at him. 'No, thank you. I do not want to play nursemaid to a visiting professor, no matter how brilliant he is. That is not my idea of fun.'

Ethan half listened to Melody as she kept talking, still feeling guilty about driving CJ from her own home. He knew she left because of him. He felt it. If she stayed home, she would hibernate in her bedroom and if she was getting up for her usual three a.m. snacks, he wasn't hearing her.

When she was out this late, he found it almost impossible to work until she was safe at home. He was conscious of her whenever she walked into the house, regardless of whether or not he was in the same room. It didn't matter where she was, he *felt* her and it was driving him insane.

Where was she? He stared out the window and when a set of headlights flashed as they turned into the driveway, he quickly stepped back into the shadows, his whole body relaxing with relief. She was back. She was safe. She was home.

Home?

He brushed the thought from his mind as he quickly headed into his part of the house, not wanting to be in her way. He listened, though, as she opened and closed the front door before making her way into the kitchen. He'd left a meal for her in the fridge and soon he heard the microwave going. Another ten minutes later and everything fell silent. She was safely down her end of the house and he was in his. His sister had hung up, giving up on him not carrying his end of the conversation.

Instead, Ethan sat down at the desk in his

room and began to get some work done. Now that CJ was safe at home, he could concentrate.

CJ finished eating the lovely food Ethan had cooked and put the dish on her bedside table, lying back in her bed and patting her baby. 'There you go. All fed for now.' Part of her had wanted him to be in the kitchen when she'd arrived home so that she could tell him about her conversation with Donna regarding Margaret. She'd also wanted to see Ethan for more than two minutes together so they could have an open and honest conversation about what on earth was happening between them.

CJ shuffled off the bed, the pain in her back beginning to intensify. She took her dishes quietly out to the kitchen, moving slowly and carefully, constantly on alert in case she should bump into him. The problem was that even if he came out, even if she asked the questions, she doubted whether either of them would have any answers. She certainly didn't and that's why she was happy to live in avoidance land for a bit longer.

Returning to her part of the house, she continued to rub the pain that was still niggling at her back. 'Did I eat too fast?' she asked the baby, wondering if she was getting referred indigestion pain, but that made no sense. The next moment she stopped in the middle of the hallway, leaning on the wall, as a sharp spasm gripped her lower abdomen. CJ gasped in shock and waited desperately for the pain to subside.

'Ow.' She rubbed her back and her abdomen. 'What was that for? Do you want some chocolate spread?' CJ headed to the stash of food she'd taken to keeping in her room. That way, she hadn't risked waking Ethan when she needed an early morning snack.

Before she could pull the chocolate spread from the bag, another pain gripped her, marginally worse than before. She sat down on the chair and felt instant discomfort, so stood once more, rubbing her belly until the pain eased. 'Just excessive back pain and Braxton-Hicks,' she told herself calmly. It meant things were definitely moving in the right direction. She would brush her teeth, then re-check her hospital bag was packed and call Donna. Although CJ was a doctor, although she'd assisted with many a delivery, reading about a contraction and experiencing one were two very different things. If this was just false labour, at least Donna would be able to put her mind at ease. As she walked to her en suite, another spasm hit.

It was then she felt a loosening sensation before a trickle of water slid down her leg. Her eyes widened in alarm as she rushed to the bathroom and stepped into the shower.

'What?' She wasn't sure what to do so she just stood there, waiting for the liquid to stop running down her legs. 'Oh, my gosh,' she whispered. 'This isn't a false alarm. This is *it*!' She was in labour.

Trembling, she thumped on the wall. 'Ethan! Ethan!' She waited, not knowing whether he could hear her. The trickle was slowing down and she started to relax a little. 'Ethan!' she called again, and thumped some more on the wall, concern in her tone.

'CJ?'

She breathed a sigh of relief. He'd heard her. 'Ethan.' He knocked on her bedroom door, which she thought was cute. 'Come in. Come in. I'm in the bathroom.' A moment later, he stood in the doorway.

'What's wrong? Why are you standing in the shower fully clothed?'

'My water—' She broke off on a gasp as another spasm hit. She closed her eyes and clenched her teeth, bracing one hand on the shower wall and the other on her abdomen.

'You're in labour?' When she looked at him, it was to find him staring at her in stunned disbelief.

CHAPTER TEN

'ARE YOU SURE? You still have a few weeks to go.'

'Tell that to the baby.' She would have laughed if she could. As it was, she concentrated on the pain, which seemed to be getting stronger as well as longer. Finally, it subsided and she relaxed against the shower wall, opening her eyes to look at him.

'I'll call Donna and the hospital and, uh…let them know we'll be over soon.' He reached into his pocket for his smartphone. 'Has it stopped?'

'Yes.'

He pressed some buttons on the phone. 'Let's see how far apart your contractions are.' He stayed with her, quickly calling Donna and then the hospital to give them the latest update. 'No doubt,' he stated after ending the call, 'the entire district will know you're in labour before we even make it across the road to the hospital.' She was still standing in the shower, her eyes closed as she rested her head against the tiles. 'Has the next contraction started?'

'No.' The instant the word left her lips the pain returned. 'I'll change my answer—yes!'

'Just over three minutes.' He waited with her

until he thought the pain had subsided. 'Settling down?'

Her eyes snapped open and she glared at him.

'Ah… I'll take that as a no.' He waited until she was finished, starting his watch again. 'I'll help you through the house and into the car.'

'No car. Can't sit down. I'll walk.'

'You want to walk to the hospital?'

'It's across the road. The car will take longer.'

'I don't know if it's a good idea.'

'Then I'll be having it here because I *can't sit down*!' she shouted.

'All right. Sure. We'll walk.' He held out his hand to her and when she didn't take it he levelled her with a warning glare. 'Accept my help, CJ. I want to give it and, more importantly, you need it.'

'Fine.'

He laughed, the rich sound washing over her in waves of happiness. How was it possible that she could feel so happy and so cross with him at the same time? She knew the thought wasn't worth dwelling on, so placed her hand in his as he helped her from the shower cubicle.

'I know you'd probably feel better if you change but let's get you over the road first. Someone can come back for clothes and things like that later.'

'My bag is packed,' she said, and motioned to the small suitcase by her bed. 'Just pick it up.'

She waved her hand impatiently in the direction
of the bag. 'Oh, and grab my food bag, too. It's
next to it.'

'Food bag?' Ethan grabbed the bags she was
pointing to and quickly peered inside the second
one. 'Chocolate spread, pickles and bananas. No
wonder I haven't heard you in the kitchen.'

'I didn't want to wake you.'

'Hmm.'

'What's that supposed to mean?' she asked an-
grily as they headed out the front door.

'Nothing.' He knew better than to start a discussion with a woman who was in this much
pain. 'Whatever makes things easier for you.'

'Oh, how magnanimous of you,' she retorted,
and Ethan chuckled.

'It doesn't matter what I say at the moment,
you're going to bite my head off and that's perfectly fine.'

CJ started to whimper but it ended up being a
silly sort of chuckle. 'I'm sorry, I'm just—'

'You don't need to apologise, or explain.' They
went slowly, taking small but steady steps, out
the front door and across the lawn. They'd just
crossed the road when the next contraction hit.

'Right on time,' Ethan announced. CJ gripped
his arm tightly as she closed her eyes and concentrated through the pain. Neither of them
moved until it was over. 'The duration of the
contraction is increasing.'

'Tell me about it.'

He let go of her hand and flexed his fingers. 'Just getting the blood flowing again, ready for next time.'

CJ laughed, then was overcome by a sense of gratitude. 'Thank you, Ethan. Thank you for helping me.'

'Hey, no problem.' He took her hand once more, the other still carrying her bags. 'The ground's a bit uneven here.' They started off again, little baby steps, slowly getting closer to the hospital. Not far from the front door she gripped his hand and leaned in closer. Ethan put the bags down and rubbed her back with his other hand, hoping it did something to bring her relief. He felt utterly helpless and wasn't really sure what he should or shouldn't be doing, but as she wasn't yelling at him, he took this as a good sign.

The night CNC came rushing out with a wheelchair. Ethan shook his head. 'CJ prefers to walk.'

'I don't *prefer* it,' she snapped as the contraction eased. 'I *can't* sit down.'

'Walking will help speed up the labour,' Bonnie told her, as she took the bags from Ethan.

'I think it's moving along pretty fast all by itself.'

'Good. Donna's on her way. Let's get you inside and see what's happening.'

They made a stop-start procession up the corridor, with CJ having another contraction in the middle. She leaned her head against Ethan's shoulder and he rubbed her back soothingly. When it passed, the sister led her into the delivery room. The bed had a floral, frilly spread on it with several throw cushions, making it seem more homely.

CJ had delivered several babies in this room, had walked passed it several times and had always thought it looked very pretty. Now…she wanted to hurl the cushions at the window and rake the feminine cover from the bed. She was in pain and the last thing she wanted was pretty, relaxing things around her.

Where were the drugs?

Oh, it was wonderful that Donna was on her way, that Ethan and the night CNC were being ever so attentive, but where was the anaesthetist? He was the one who could give her some pain relief, an epidural—anything.

'Charlie. Ring Charlie,' she said.

'I've already called him. He's on his way.'

CJ glared at Bonnie. 'Go and get him *now*.'

'I'll settle her in,' Ethan remarked, noticing the surprised look on Bonnie's face.

'I don't need *anyone* to settle me,' CJ added. 'I'm fine. Women have babies all the time and now it's my turn and I'm *fine*!'

'Yes, you are,' Ethan pacified as he tossed the

cushions off the bed onto a chair and pulled the bedspread back. CJ smirked in a self-satisfied way at the inanimate objects, glad of his rough treatment of them. He wound the bed down so it was easier for her to get on but she found she couldn't.

'Can't lie down either.' She looked at him, her eyes beginning to fill with tears. 'I can't sit down, I can't lie down and my legs are aching and tired.'

'I know. I know,' he soothed. 'Lean on me.' He gathered her near so her head was resting on his shoulder.

'I'm sorry if I'm being horrible.'

He laughed. 'You're not.'

'Liar.'

He laughed again. 'Probably.'

She pulled back to look at him, her terrified green eyes meeting his sympathetic blue ones. 'Thank you,' she whispered.

Ethan felt a knot of tension, need and anger churn in his gut. Tension because he was fighting as hard as he could against the attraction. Need because it was becoming impossible *not* to give in and kiss her, and anger against her husband for leaving her to cope with this experience all alone.

She was an amazing woman and his feelings for her were intensifying with every moment he spent in her company. It wasn't right. He knew that, but he also knew the wrong thing could sometimes feel so right.

He swallowed over all his thoughts and emotions and bent down to kiss her forehead. 'You'll be fine.' He felt her body tense and knew another contraction was on the way. He helped her through it, his eyes closed as they leaned against each other, both concentrating on what was happening. When he opened his eyes, it was to find Donna standing in the doorway, watching them.

'Good evening. You look as though you're having loads of fun.' She came in and patted CJ lightly on the shoulder. 'Right. Has anyone checked the baby yet?'

Ethan waited for CJ to answer but when she didn't, he shook his head.

'Can you get up on the bed?'

'Too uncomfortable,' she mumbled.

'OK. Stay where you are, I'll work around you.' For the next ten minutes there were people in and out of the room, the baby's heartbeat was checked and found to be perfect. CJ was given a once-over by Donna and pronounced to be almost nine centimetres dilated.

'That's very quick. Hang on, your sister had quick labours with her children, didn't she?'

'Four hours for the first and two hours for the second,' CJ said softly between contractions. 'Looks as though you might break her record.'

Donna chuckled. 'I was in labour for over fifteen hours and that was with my last one.'

'Where's Charlie?'

'I'll go check.' Donna headed out, leaving CJ leaning on Ethan, closing her eyes as she tried to rest between contractions. It was a good half an hour later before Charlie walked in the door and by that time CJ was fully dilated.

'Where have you been?' she growled at the anaesthetist when he gave her a cheery greeting.

'It's always nice to feel so appreciated,' Charlie joked as he read CJ's chart, checking that both mother and baby were doing well. 'OK. You have no allergies so let me go get you some—'

Before Charlie could finish his sentence, CJ had another contraction but this one gripped her abdomen even tighter and, quite involuntarily, she gave a push.

'Was that a push?' Donna asked. They all waited and when CJ involuntarily pushed again, Charlie chuckled.

'Well, you don't need me any more,' he joked.

'Yes. Yes, I do.' CJ grabbed him by the front of his shirt and dragged his face closer. 'Give me something. Anything!'

'I can't, CJ. You know that.'

'The window has closed?'

'The window has closed,' Charlie confirmed.

'Open a door,' she whimpered, and let go of his shirt.

'CJ.' Charlie smoothed a comforting hand over her forehead. 'You'll be fine. The baby's fine. There seems to be an abundance of people in here, so I'll be in the kitchen if you need me.'

CJ reached out a hand but he was gone. Her window was shut and so was the door. Why couldn't he open it again? She stuck out her lower lip. 'I don't want to do this any more.'

Donna laughed. 'You're doing a great job and the fact that you're saying you want to go home proves that everything is moving along nicely.' When the next contraction gripped, CJ pushed again. She rested her head on Ethan's shoulder between contractions and closed her eyes, conserving what energy she had.

It seemed to take for ever but three hours later Donna told her to give one more push and the head was finally out. The cord wasn't around the neck and they waited while the shoulders rotated. CJ had managed to get comfortable on a beanbag as her legs had eventually given up supporting her.

Ethan held her hand tightly, dabbing her forehead with a damp cloth. She hadn't wanted him to go and he'd made no move to leave. Now... they were almost finished and she could hardly believe the man she'd known for only a few weeks had stayed to help her through this.

CJ knew it was ridiculous but…she loved him. Whether it was the love of a lifetime or a love of utter gratitude, she had no way of knowing. Perhaps it was the hormones or the intimacy of their present situation but her feelings would not be repressed. The next contraction started to grip and she squeezed his hand once more.

'That's it. Good girl. Keep going, CJ,' Donna coached. 'Snatch a breath—one more push and—'

CJ felt the baby leave her and was amazed at the immediate sense of loss. The intimacy only *she* could share with her child was over. Everything was silent for a second or two and she didn't even realise that Ethan had let go of her hand to quickly assist Donna—and then it came. The most glorious sound in the entire world— the cry of a newborn babe.

Donna placed the child into CJ's waiting arms. 'You have a daughter.'

The loss she'd just felt vanished into thin air as she held her little girl for the very first time, kissing the soft, downy head.

'Oh, baby.' Her eyes filled with tears that spilled over. 'Baby, you're here.'

'What are you going to call her?' The question came from Ethan, his voice not quite so steady. CJ looked up to see his own eyes glistening with tears. She reached out a hand to him, which he took, drawing him closer.

'Ethan...' Her throat was scratchy and sore and with the swell of emotion she felt, it was no wonder it was hard to speak.

'Really? I think you can think of a prettier name than that,' he whispered with a soft chuckle.

She laughed and swallowed. 'Will you help me?'

'Name her?' When she nodded, he smiled. 'I'd be delighted and honoured.'

The child in her arms slept, their gazes held and slowly but surely he moved in closer. The kiss he pressed on her lips was the most natural thing he'd ever done. The feeling of coming home was the most natural feeling he'd ever felt.

And he was at a loss to explain why neither terrified him.

'Have you come up with any more names?' Donna asked as she came around to check on CJ. CJ was sitting in bed, propped up by pillows, feeding her beautiful daughter. 'Everyone's on tenterhooks to find out what you'll call her, and discover who has won the competition.'

'Who picked the right date?'

'Idris at the supermarket. Robert chose the correct time of birth so now we're just waiting on the name.'

CJ chuckled. 'I love the way they all get involved.'

'I can't believe she's two days old and you still haven't even thought of a name.'

'I want to find one that suits her. I liked Susan yesterday but…' She trailed off and shook her head.

'Has Ethan been in this morning?'

'Not yet but we're expecting him soon.' The baby had finished feeding and CJ sat her up to burp her. 'Aren't we a beautiful girl. We're expecting Ethan really soon. Yes, we are. Oh, you're so precious.' CJ kissed her daughter's head, breathing in the scent and filing the memory away for later. Once the baby had released her wind, CJ re-wrapped the gorgeous girl in a blanket. 'I like the name Joy. Are you a Joy?' She smiled. 'Yes. Yes you are a joy, an absolute joy.'

'Joy?' Ethan queried as he strode into the room. 'Joy Nicholls. Has a ring to it. I gather you've given up Susan?'

'Yes. I don't think she looks like a Susan any more.'

'What about… Elizabeth?'

CJ watched as he scooped the baby up into his arms as though it were the most natural thing in the world. He kissed her head and rubbed his cheek against her softness, breathing that gorgeous baby scent in the same way CJ had.

'Elizabeth. Elizabeth Nicholls.' She mulled

it over. 'I quite like it. Elizabeth. Does she look like an Elizabeth, Ethan?'

He studied the little girl who was going to sleep in his arms. 'You know, I think she does. And also I like Lizzie, for when she's cheeky and mischievous.'

'Where did you get Elizabeth from?' Donna asked.

'It was my great-grandmother's name,' Ethan stated.

'It's very pretty.'

'We need something that goes with Elizabeth,' Ethan continued, rocking the baby gently from side to side. CJ liked watching him hold the baby, liked the way he looked with the little girl in his arms, liked the way he'd just *loved* her so unconditionally. She'd been worried that being at the birth, helping her, holding the baby—all of it would have brought back horrible memories for him but, in fact, it was the opposite. It was as though Elizabeth's birth had helped him to heal. Still, CJ was cautious. There were still too many questions in the air surrounding Ethan, herself and the baby, but for now, naming the gorgeous girl was enough to deal with.

They all thought. 'What about Janice?' Donna asked.

CJ pondered, then shook her head.

'What about Jean?' Ethan suggested. 'After

you, Claudia-Jean. You could hyphenate her name, too.'

'EJ and CJ? Well, the Jean part of my name was after my mother so that way Elizabeth would be named after both of us.' She laughed.

'And she deserves to carry the family name—your name,' he continued. 'You did an amazing job, bringing her into this world.' He looked at the baby. 'Elizabeth-Jean Nicholls.'

'It's pretty,' Donna remarked. She looked from one to the other. 'Decided?'

CJ smiled at Ethan. 'Decided. Elizabeth-Jean she is.'

'This calls for a celebration,' Donna said, and headed off to tell the rest of the staff. After Donna had left the room, CJ peered at her daughter.

'Is she asleep?'

'Yes.'

'Do you want to put her down?'

'No.' He smiled sheepishly and sat down on the bed next to CJ. 'I like holding her.'

'Me too. I was supposed to put her in her cot last night but I just didn't want to let her go so I slept with her in my arms all night long. Snuggled together.' Her smile was bright and she sighed with happiness.

'So how are you feeling today?'

'Better.'

Ethan angled Elizabeth up in his arms so they

could both look at the baby's sleeping face. 'She's beautiful, CJ. Simply beautiful.'

'She is, isn't she,' CJ whispered rhetorically, brushing her finger lightly over Elizabeth's cheek. 'I can't believe how perfectly I love her. I didn't know she was missing from my life until she was here.' She chuckled and looked at him. 'I don't know if that makes any sense at all.'

'It does.' He turned his head and returned her gaze. 'Perfect sense.' As they continued to look at each other, the atmosphere in the room intensified, the awareness between them growing with every passing second they spent together. Where prior to Elizabeth's birth they'd been able to keep their distance, the experience they'd shared—the miracle of life—seemed to have made the bond even stronger. CJ's lips parted and her breathing increased as she continued to gaze into Ethan's eyes. He made her feel so wonderful, so cherished, so strong and she wanted desperately to kiss him, to show him how much she appreciated his care and support.

Without a word spoken, he leaned forward and placed his lips on hers as though it were the most natural thing in the world. It was like the first kiss they'd shared, feather-light and very brief, then he shifted back slightly and cleared his throat. As she looked at him for a moment longer, she could clearly see his concern, his questions and his confusion. She didn't blame him as she felt the same way. Now, however, was not the time for such a discussion and they both knew it, hence she also understood why he hadn't made the effort to deepen the kiss.

'Er…the nurses mentioned that you're planning to discharge yourself and Elizabeth tomorrow.' He looked down at the baby as he spoke and the moment of repressed need and desire vanished.

'Yes. I'd like to get home and settled into a routine. I'm not far from the hospital, both you and Donna will be across the road at the clinic during the day should we need anything, and you'll be in the house in the evening. I don't see any reason to stay and take up a hospital bed.'

'I'm not criticising you, I'm merely making a statement. The reason I made the statement is that I was also told about the hospital's custom.'

'Custom?'

'Well, it can't be a very good one if their own GP doesn't know about it.'

'Which one?'

'The one where the new mother is taken out to dinner for a few hours the night before she returns home. A celebration for her hard labour.' He raised his eyebrows on the pun.

'Oh. *That* custom.' CJ had forgotten about it, simply because she had no one to take her out. Was Ethan suggesting that *he* was going to take her out? Tingles of excitement buzzed through her. 'Why do you…er…mention it?' Maybe he was offering to look after Elizabeth while she went out to dinner by herself or with some of her friends.

'Because I want to take you to dinner. You deserve it.'

'Dinner?' she repeated. 'Uh…where were you thinking of going?'

'I hadn't actually thought that far. Do you have any suggestions? Favourite places? Or would you like to be surprised?'

'Um…' She couldn't think. She hadn't been out to dinner in such a very long time she wasn't sure what to say. 'Surprise me.'

'OK. Surprise it is.' His smile was wide and encompassing.

'Are you looking forward to this more than me?' As she asked the question, she saw a hint of sadness creep into Ethan's gaze. He looked down at Elizabeth for a moment, brushing a kiss to the baby's head.

'It's also my way of thanking you for allow-ing me to be a part of your miracle.'

Tears instantly sprang to CJ's eyes and she placed her hand on his arm. 'If the experiences of the last few days have helped bring you some level of healing for your past pain, then I'm very happy.'

Ethan raised his gaze to meet hers briefly and he nodded, then looked at the clock on the wall. 'I have to go or I'll be late for clinic.' He handed her the baby, their arms and hands touching briefly—but it was enough for them both to stop, stare at each other, then mumble muffled apologies. 'Enjoy your steady stream of visitors.'

'We will. They'll all be even more thrilled now that she has a name.'

'See you at seven tonight.'

CJ watched him go, then looked at her sleeping babe. She shuffled down in the bed, discarding pillows as she went until finally she and Elizabeth were snuggled up together. 'I love you, Lizzie-Jean,' she whispered, and kissed the downy forehead. People may come and go from her life, like her parents and her husband—and even Ethan, who would one day return to Sydney. Now, though, she had someone of her own, filling a void in her life she hadn't known existed. Whatever happened or didn't happen between her and Ethan, CJ vowed to be the best mother ever, to always love her little girl.

But it would be wonderful if the man who, she was sure, loved Elizabeth as much as she did could find it in his heart to love her, too.

'That would be perfect,' she whispered to her daughter, before drifting off to sleep.

CHAPTER ELEVEN

'No DINNER FOR you tonight,' Donna remarked as she waltzed into CJ's room carrying a garment bag.

'Pardon?' For one heart-stopping moment, CJ thought Ethan had cancelled.

'From the hospital kitchen, I mean.'

'Whew!' She placed her hand over her heart. 'Don't *do* that to me.'

Donna laughed. 'Sorry. Here. I brought you a surprise.' She held out the garment bag. 'It's my present to you.'

CJ unzipped the bag and gasped as she took out a breath-taking black dress. It was simple, elegant, and one that she'd admired at an online boutique for months. She looked from the dress to Donna. 'How did you do it? Ethan only asked me this morning to go out to dinner.'

'I called the online shop and had them express deliver it.'

'What! You shouldn't have gone to so much bother.'

'Nonsense. You deserve this night.'

CJ could feel the tears brimming in her eyes. She put the dress on the bed and rushed to hug her friend. 'Thank you. Thank you so much.'

'Hey, don't start crying now. Ethan's going to be here in half an hour and we don't want your face all blotchy.'

CJ sniffed and smiled. 'You're right.' She picked up the dress and held it against her before turning to Elizabeth, who was sleeping in the hospital cot. 'Look, princess. Does Mummy look pretty?'

'Mummy looks sickeningly good,' Donna said. 'I wish my figure had sprung back as quickly as yours. I don't know. You have an easy and quick labour and a few days later you're almost back to what you were before you became pregnant. It's just not fair.'

CJ laughed. 'I can't help it.'

'No. Although I would like to add that when you get pregnant again—some time in the future—we keep a close eye on you when you go into labour because, boy, oh, boy, do you go quickly. You'll be lucky to make it across the road to the hospital with the next one.'

'What *next one*?' she scoffed, but didn't dwell on it. 'I want to enjoy the baby I have because before I know it she'll be on her way to university.'

'Don't I know it!' Donna laughed. 'All right. Ethan's going to be here soon so let's get you organised.' She pulled out a large bag with cosmetics, a hairdryer, curler and hair spray, and a pair of stockings. 'I stopped by your house earlier to pick up a pair of shoes for you but the back door was locked.'

'Ethan.' CJ shrugged and shook her head. 'He's a stickler for locking the doors.'

'I figured as much. You get changed and I'll pop over and get a pair now. He should be home but give me your keys in case he's still at the clinic.'

When she'd gone, CJ slipped out of her pyjamas and pulled on the dress. The straps were two inches wide in a zig-zag pattern with a row of diamantés in the middle. The neckline also had a zig-zag pattern that came across the top of the bust, glittering diamantés again highlighting the unusual cut. It came to mid-thigh and showed off her legs to perfection.

Thankfully, Donna had bought the next size up from what CJ usually wore so when she zipped it up, it didn't pull across her bust. She'd already expressed milk after the last feed just in case Elizabeth should wake up hungry while she was gone.

She looked down at her sleeping daughter. 'Oh, baby. You are so beautiful. Sleep well while I'm gone. I'll be back. I promise. I will *never* leave you and I will *love* you for ever.'

Donna rushed back into the room, stopping still as she gazed at CJ. She shook her head. 'Even without the hair and make-up, you look incredible. He isn't going to know what hit him!'

They set to work, piling CJ's hair on top of her head and curling the ends slightly, leaving a few loose tendrils coming down. 'I have another surprise,' Donna announced after she'd finished CJ's make-up. She pulled out a jeweller's box. 'I wore these on my wedding day and they've never been worn since.' Donna handed it to CJ, who opened it slowly. A row of diamonds winked back at her. The necklace was a classically simple strand with matching bracelet and a pair of studded earrings.

'Oh! I can't.'

'You owe it to the jewels. They deserve to be seen and they match the dress perfectly. Now, no more fuss. Turn around so I can fasten these in place.'

CJ did what Donna told her to do, as her hair and make-up were completed. When she stood and looked in the half-mirror of the hospital bathroom, she barely recognised herself.

'You really do look like a princess,' Donna stated. 'Please, have a great time.'

'I feel so spoilt.'

'You deserve it. You've given so much to this town, it's time we all gave something back.'

CJ smoothed a hand down the dress and smiled brightly at her reflection. Tonight, she decided, was a night of hope and she determined to enjoy *everything* it offered.

* * *

Ethan drove his car to the hospital, furious with himself for being late.

He'd called Bonnie to let her know the clinic had run late and to pass on a message to CJ. It was almost seven-thirty! He parked the car, cut the engine and rushed into the hospital. When he arrived at CJ's room, it was to find her dressed in a robe, sitting up in bed, feeding Elizabeth. He stopped and stared, their gazes meeting.

Her hair was on top of her head in a pile of curls, her face had make-up on it and diamonds seem to twinkle around her neck and ears. She looked…sexy! Wholesome, and irresistibly sexy. He swallowed over the dryness of his throat.

'Sorry. She woke up and was hungry, so I thought it would be best to feed her before we go. Will this affect your plans for this evening?'

He gulped as he took a few steps into the room, then stopped. The urge to crush her to him and plunder her mouth was almost too great for him to control. He swallowed again.

'No. I've called the restaurant to let them know but they understand how it is and will hold the table for as long as we need.'

'Good. She's almost finished.'

The room was plunged into silence again and CJ began to feel a little uncomfortable. Why didn't he come into the room? Sit down? Say something? She glanced up at him, only to find him intently watching them. When Elizabeth had finished her feed, CJ closed her robe and handed him the baby.

'Here's a towel. Would you mind burping her while I go and get changed?'

'Sure.' He walked to the bed and sat on the end, glad CJ was leaving the room for a moment. Hopefully, he'd be able to get himself under control again. 'You're worse than your mother,' he muttered to Elizabeth as he rubbed her back soothingly. 'Irresistible and highly kissable.' He pressed his lips to her head. Once she'd finished, he wrapped her up and tucked her into the cot. Then he concentrated on taking some deep, calming breaths. He was determined to be in control of his faculties when Elizabeth's mother returned.

'Ready?'

Ethan spun around and simply stared at the woman who stood in the doorway. Where had *she* come from? CJ felt as if he'd never seen her before. Dressed in the most stunning of black dresses, with diamonds everywhere and long, luscious legs. His jaw dropped open and he felt paralysed with desire.

'Claudia-Jean...you are *stunning*,' he breathed, and, finally able to move his legs, he walked to her side. 'Ready?' He crooked his arm for her to take.

'Thank you.' She smiled up at him and he almost capitulated. The urge to sweep her into his arms and carry her back to their house was increasing at an alarming rate.

'Ready to go?' It was Bonnie who broke the spell as she walked down the corridor towards them.

CJ cleared her throat and looked away first. 'Yes. She's fed, burped, clean nappy and sleeping like a baby.' Bonnie wheeled the cot down to the nurses' station as the two of them walked behind. CJ blew her girl a kiss. 'Sleep sweet, princess.'

Ethan led her out to the car and for once she was glad he'd put up the soft top. 'Are you going to be warm enough?'

'Yes. From the hospital to the car, to the restaurant, to the car, to the hospital. I should be fine.' He walked her around to the passenger side and held the door for her. 'Thank you.'

'Where are we going?' she asked as they drove along, the scent of his aftershave winding itself around her.

'Chateau Cregg.'

'Oh, they have a lovely restaurant there, or so I've heard.'

'Never been?'

'No.'

He smiled. 'I'm delighted tonight is the first time.'

They were met at the door by the maître d' then shown to their table. She smiled across the table at him, determined to enjoy every moment they had together. They talked on a variety of topics while they ate. Ethan told her a few stories from his childhood and the silly things he, his brother and sister had done. She was able to counter a few of them with crazy tales about herself and her sister. After dessert, they made their way back to the car.

'It's been a lovely evening.' CJ sighed wistfully as Ethan pulled away from the restaurant. 'Thank you, Ethan. You can't know how much a night out like this means to me. In fact, I can't recall ever having been out on a night like tonight.'

'I'm really glad to hear that. I had a good time, too.'

'How long is it since *you've* been out on night like this?'

Ethan slowly shook his head. 'Far too long to even remember.'

He changed gear and indicated to turn. 'If I hadn't had a mild heart attack, I would never have come here. I would never have met the people of these districts, seen the way they all seem to look after each other.' He glanced across at her for a quick moment. 'I never would have met you and I never would have been privileged to experience Elizabeth's birth. To see her so...complete.' He nodded. 'It's how it should be.'

'Yes. She is rather awesome.' It was then that CJ looked out the car window and realised they weren't headed back to the hospital. 'Where are we going?'

'To the lookout.'

'Oh?'

'Donna mentioned it today and as I haven't managed to get here yet, and as it's sort of on the way back to the hospital, I thought you wouldn't mind stopping and taking in the sight with me.'

'No, I don't mind. It really is beautiful, especially on a clear night like tonight.'

'And we have an almost full moon.'

CJ grinned. 'So we do. A full moon. A clear night. If I was working in a city hospital emergency department, I'd be worried.' They both chuckled at her words. 'Out here, the same night holds a different purpose.'

'And what purpose is that?'

'That anything can happen.'

Ethan nodded, then drove up a small hill and parked in the car park before coming around to her side to help her out.

'I'm not pregnant any more, Ethan. I can get out of the car by myself.'

'I know...but a gentleman always escorts his date.'

'Is that what I am tonight? Your date?'

204 FALLING FOR THE PREGNANT GP

'Absolutely, m'lady.'

CJ giggled as he led her over the low stone wall that ringed the car park. 'I think the last time I went on an actual date was…probably high school.'

'Well, tonight you're with me and that's all I care about.'

'Is it?'

He looked down into her face. 'Right now, yes.' He brushed his fingertips across her cheek. 'You really do look extraordinarily beautiful tonight, Claudia-Jean.'

'Thank you.' She dipped her head slightly, hoping he wouldn't see how much his words had pleased her. 'You don't scrub up too badly yourself.'

'You've seen me in a suit lots of times.'

'Yes, but tonight you're looking… I don't know…different. Handsome different.'

Ethan quirked an eyebrow. 'I don't look handsome at other times?'

She laughed. 'That's not what I meant and you know it. There's something…different about you tonight. I think it might be more in your eyes, rather than what you're wearing.'

His gaze was intense. 'I don't want to hurt you,' he said softly, and CJ's heart was pierced by his tenderness. Again, he brushed her cheek with his hand before cupping her face and drawing it closer to his own. When his lips met hers, CJ sighed into the kiss.

His mouth was soft, gentle, as though she'd break if he exerted any more force. He made her feel precious, treasured and...loved. Was she insane to hope that one day Ethan would come to care for her as deeply as she cared for him?

After a moment, he gently pulled away and gazed at her before gathering her closer in his arms. When he felt the coolness of her skin he pulled back, took his jacket off and draped it over her shoulders. 'Not that I want to cover up your exquisite dress but neither do I want you to get sick. Bonnie, not to mention Donna, would have my hide.'

CJ nodded but was unable to speak. The emotions he evoked in her were so overpowering, so overwhelming she wasn't quite sure how to cope with them. Instead, she took delight in being drawn into his embrace, of resting her head against his chest and savouring the scent of him. She closed her eyes, memorising everything she could, filing it away to take out one day in the future when her life might not be so perfect as it was at this moment.

'The stars in Sydney don't shine as brightly as here.'

'Yet they're the same stars,' she murmured, opening her eyes and shifting away a little. She couldn't look at him. She didn't want to think about Sydney, or the fact that he had a life there—a life without her.

He must have sensed a change in her mood because he whispered, 'I don't want to hurt you, CJ.'

'So you've said.' She pulled back and stepped from his embrace, tugging the edges of his jacket around her. She turned her back to him and tilted her head back to look at the stars. Ethan left her for a moment, desperate to get his own thoughts and emotions under control. Where he never thought he'd come to care so deeply for another woman, here he was, desperate to throw everything away just to stay with her and Elizabeth. He *wanted* to be in their lives, he *wanted* to do whatever it took to ensure both of them remained happy and healthy for the rest of their days. Even the realisation of the thoughts he'd been doing his best to hold at bay was enough to scare him.

He had a life in Sydney, a career. Was that enough for him now? He didn't know. All he was certain of was that Claudia-Jean Nicholls had become incredibly special to him in a matter of weeks! It was impossible, yet here he was, experiencing these emotions.

His only rationalisation was that because he'd shut his heart away for so long, because he'd denied himself the ability to truly interact with other people, the first time he'd stepped back into the light he'd fallen hard for a woman who was so different from every other woman he'd ever known. She'd been open and honest with him, listening to him, sharing her life with him. Not only was she exquisitely stunning, she was generous and kind.

'CJ.' At her name, she turned and glanced at him. He closed the distance between them and placed his hands on her shoulders, both of them staring at the stars for a moment before she slowly turned in his arms to look up at him. She was so brave. She'd overcome so much in her life and was still willing to face the future head on, regardless of what it held. He lowered his mouth to hers, intent on showing her that he cared.

He kept the kisses soft, caressing her mouth with his, wanting to convey just how much he cherished her. When she responded to him, giving herself to him, something deep inside seemed to surge to the surface and he wrapped his arms around her, needing her as close as possible. He wanted this woman. The desire was so powerful, so strong he had no idea how to control it, which was definitely a first for him. He seemed to be experiencing a lot of 'firsts' with CJ and the sensations were knocking him off balance far more than he liked. Still, there was nothing he could do about it—especially when he was holding her so close.

Her scent had wrapped itself around him, in much the same way as his arms were wrapped around her. How could this feel so right when, for a multitude of logical reasons, it was so wrong? They were locked together in an electrifying embrace, one so hot he was sure they'd sizzle and steam if the heavens opened up and poured rain on them.

Still, she matched the intensity of his kisses, as though she was desperate to show him she wanted this as much as he did. Never in her life had she felt this way. Her appetite for him appeared to be voracious and uncontrollable. How in the world was she supposed to let this man go? She knew it was inevitable, she knew the day would come when he would walk away from her. She wouldn't think about that now, not when his mouth was hot on hers, not when her heart was pounding with unbelievable joy. She needed to enjoy this moment in time. This was what she'd craved almost since the first moment she'd laid eyes on him.

He shifted slightly and brought first one arm, then the other beneath the jacket on her shoulders, ensuring it didn't fall off with the movement. He groaned as he slowly slid his hands around her waist, his thumbs gently caressing the underside of her breasts before continuing around to draw little circles at the base of her spine. Now there was only one barrier separating him from the touch of her skin and for the moment he could live with that.

He broke free, just for a second, both of them breathing heavily, their hearts beating in a wild and unsteady rhythm. He pressed small butterfly kisses to her cheek, down to her ear, where he nibbled for a brief moment before continuing down to her neck.

She arched back slightly, giving him access to what he'd been coveting for weeks. Even the necklace she wore didn't deter him, even though he wished it were gone. She laced her fingers into his hair, revelling in the fact that she was finally allowed to touch him in this familiar way, to feel the soft strands of his dark, brown locks smooth against her fingertips. His head dipped lower still, the kisses warm against the cool air that circulated around them, as he made his way to the top of her chest.

Up and down, along the zig-zag of her dress, he tenderly placed his lips, his hands now spanning her midriff, his thumbs repeating the action they'd performed earlier. She gasped as her body responded, heat burning right through her—and then she felt it. That strange, new sensation that happened to breastfeeding mothers.

'Whoa!' She quickly took two steps away, severing the embrace. 'Stop.'

'What?' He looked at her with dazed confusion. 'Are you all right? I didn't hurt you?' He took a step closer and reached out a hand to her.

CJ melted at his concern and smiled, putting her hand in his.

'I'm fine. Really, I'm fine.' She sucked in air, trying to steady her heart rate, but she was feeling the cold without his body there to shield her. 'It's just that...' She took a steadying breath. 'I'm...' Oh, this was so embarrassing. 'I'm... leaking.'

She watched as his eyes flicked to her breasts in alarm before meeting her gaze once more. A smile started to twitch at the corner of his lips as he squeezed her hand.

'Yes. Um...sorry.'

She watched him carefully, unsure *what* he was apologising for. 'Don't apologise. I guess I'm just not used to...well...everything.'

'I think we both got a little carried away.' He raked his free hand through his hair where her own fingers had been only moments ago.

CJ laughed. 'This is certainly a memorable end to the evening.'

'Yes.' When he saw her shiver, he escorted her to the car. 'Pumpkin time.'

'Yes,' she agreed, glad of the car's instant warmth from the wind. He walked around to the driver's side and climbed in. He started the engine, switching on the heater, but didn't make any move to drive.

'It really is beautiful up here.'

'It's one of my favourite spots.'

'I can see why. The whole area, what I've seen of it, is charming.'

'But…?'

'But it's not my home.'

'I know.'

'I don't want you to think I'm taking advantage of you because that's not my intention.'

'I know that, too. The attraction between us is real and sometimes…' she shrugged '…uncontrollable.'

'You can say that again,' he mumbled, and shook his head. 'I guess what I'm trying, very inarticulately, to say is that I don't want to hurt you…but I know I am.'

'Yes,' she stated. 'And I'm hurting you.'

'It can't work.'

'I know. You have your life. I have mine.' A small smile touched her lips. 'I have Elizabeth to consider now. She must come first in all my decisions. Not only that but I have my home, my work and my friends. In time, the way you make me feel will fade and I'll be fine. And you'll be fine. This…' she indicated the wonderful scenery before them '…was just a pleasant interlude.'

Ethan opened his mouth to say something, then thought better of it. Instead, he buckled up his seat belt, waiting until she followed suit, then started the engine. He manoeuvred the car out the exit and down the hill to the town below. Both were silent on the five-minute drive and thankfully, not a minute too soon, soon they were pulling up outside the hospital.

CJ opened her door and climbed out before he could come around to help her. She needed to do things for herself, to be completely independent. She was a mother now. She needed to be strong, determined and focused. When he stood before her, she smiled. 'Thank you again for such an amazing evening. It's one I'll never forget.'

'Nor I.' Then Ethan leaned forward and brushed his lips across hers for one final kiss. They stared at each other for a long moment, their hearts and minds so full with words neither of them would say. CJ broke eye contact first, swallowing over the lump in her throat.

'I'd better go check on Elizabeth.'

He nodded. 'Of course.'

Forcing her legs to move, she turned and walked into the hospital, determined not to look back. The pain she felt in her chest, which coursed throughout her entire body, was evidence that her heart was breaking and now there was no reason to hold back the tears.

CHAPTER TWELVE

'Hi.' CJ OPENED the door to let Donna in. 'We were going to come across to the clinic later today for the check-up. I even rang to make an appointment with Tania and she told me I was being ridiculous.'

Donna laughed as she came in and sat down at CJ's kitchen table. 'She told me. You should know by now that you don't need to make an appointment in your own practice.'

'Well, I thought I should do things by the book. You know, no preferential treatment.'

Donna laughed again. 'You really haven't been getting much sleep, have you? That's the only reason I can come up with as to why your brain's gone soft. Preferential treatment, indeed. Who else *should* get it?'

CJ gazed down at Elizabeth, sleeping peacefully in the bassinet. 'I'm actually getting more sleep now than I was before I had her.'

'Good.'

'Have you got time for a cuppa?'

'That would be lovely.'

'Busy clinic?'

Donna nodded. 'Ethan's doing the afternoon clinic and I'll do the house calls. I came across not only to check on how you were both doing but to ask if you'd like to come along.'

CJ found it hard to curb her disappointment. 'Of course,' she said softly, and forced a smile. 'We'd love to come.' She turned away and concentrated on filling the kettle and switching it on. Why did she feel like crying?

'Things still aren't going well between you and Ethan?'

CJ looked at her friend. 'No, but, then, it's no more than I expected.'

'Expected? What do you mean? I thought the night he took you out to dinner was a positive step forward. Now it seems as though you're avoiding each other again.'

'Not so much avoiding but...' She shrugged. 'Well, yes, I guess you could say avoiding.'

'What about Elizabeth?'

CJ smiled and looked at her daughter. 'He'd never ignore her. She wouldn't let him. He's happy to hold her, look after her, especially if I need to have a shower or if I'm on the phone with a patient. The other night I was sitting in the lounge, feeding her, and he came in and sat with us.'

'That's promising.'

CJ shook her head. 'He asked polite, medical questions about how she was doing, feeding and that sort of thing. When she was finished he offered to burp her and when she dozed off he checked her over—even got his stethoscope and listened to her heart—and then, when he was satisfied, he left.'

Donna's lips formed another circle. 'Oh.' The kettle boiled and switched itself off but neither of them moved. 'So what's next?'

She shrugged. 'I'm just taking things one day at a time.'

'He's here for another five months, CJ.'

'I know and I've been thinking about that. I mean, we could talk to him and see if he wants to alter his contract. He doesn't have to stay the full six months we initially agreed on.'

'You're not ready to come back to work. I won't allow it.'

'Not full time but definitely part time or even three-quarter time.'

'Three-quarter time? Will you listen to yourself? Your daughter is only two weeks old.'

'Yes, and she's a good baby. She sleeps well, she feeds well and she's no trouble at all.'

'What about breastfeeding, if you come back to work too early?'

'I've thought of that. Why couldn't I bring Elizabeth in to work with me? She can sleep in the reception area with Tania and when she needs feeding, I can sit down and feed her. Trust me,' she went on quickly, noticing the look of scepticism on Donna's face, 'the patients won't mind waiting if Elizabeth needs feeding. They all adore her and that way everyone can see her when they come to the clinic.'

'What if she needs changing? Or she's sick? Tania can't look after her. Besides, it's a medical clinic, CJ, not a child-care centre.'

'All right. How about I find someone to look after her here at home? A nanny. I'm only working across the road so I can pop home whenever I'm needed, for feeding and stuff like that.'

Donna shook her head and said softly, 'Is it really *that bad* with Ethan around? This time you have now with Elizabeth won't come again. She'll never be this little again, CJ, and I don't want you to miss it because it does go quickly. My kids are at university, living their own lives and occasionally calling their mother, yet it seems like only yesterday I was changing their nappies!'

CJ slumped forward onto the table in defeat. 'I have to find my life—my life without Ethan— and the only way I can see that happening is if he leaves. I know he's as uncomfortable with things as I am and, to be honest, I can't take any more of his extreme politeness.' She lifted her head. 'If he stays for the next five months, I'll definitely be in love with the man and then…when he goes I'll be in even worse shape than now.'

Donna watched her for a moment before getting up and switching the kettle on again. 'OK. We'll have a cuppa, talk through all possibilities and come up with a workable plan—one Ethan needs to agree to as well.'

CJ sighed with relief. 'Good. Let's do this. Let's move forward.'

The next night, when Ethan came home from the clinic, he found CJ nursing Elizabeth in the lounge room.

'Hi.'

She looked up from the child and smiled sleepily at him. 'Hi, yourself. How was clinic?'

Ethan clenched his hands into fists to stop himself from walking to her side and pressing a firm kiss to her lips. Didn't she have any idea just how wonderful she looked, all sleepy and tousled and dressed in her old robe with fluffy slippers? It was definitely not chic but it was comfortable and homey and...very CJ.

'Clinic was long,' he answered, then came further into the room and sat in the chair opposite her. There was quite a bit of distance between them, for which he was grateful. 'Uh...there's something I need to talk to you about.'

'Really? Because there's something I need to talk to you about.'

'Oh. OK. Do you want me to go first?' He'd been going over things in his head for most of the afternoon.

'Sure.'

'Well...uh...' He sighed. 'I don't think I should

live here any more. I think I'll get a place somewhere else for the duration of my contract.'

'Oh.' CJ frowned and looked down at Elizabeth, who had fallen asleep, her tummy clearly
full. She rearranged her clothing and shifted
Elizabeth onto her shoulder so she could rub the
little girl's back to help release any wind.

'I mean, it was great I was here when you went
into labour so I could help, and also for these first
few weeks. I've enjoyed being able to look after
Elizabeth when you needed me to, like when you
have a shower, but…' He stopped and bowed his
head, trying to gather his thoughts into a logical order. 'Basically, I'm too attracted to you to
stay here.'

'Wow. That's…very honest.'

'You've taught me it's the best way.'

'I have? Well, then…uh… I was going to
ask you if you actually wanted to change your
contract so that you finish sooner rather than
later. That way, you don't have to worry about
looking around for accommodation, you're not
trapped here and you can return to Sydney and
do whatever it is that you want to do there.' She
shrugged one shoulder. 'I'm sure there are several research projects that require your exper-
tise, or even new projects you'd like to get off the
ground. You did mention when we went out to
dinner that you had several prospects you were
thinking about.'

'If I finish my contract early, who will cover your patients?'

'I will.'

'What about Elizabeth?'

'I'm going to hire a nanny. I've already spoken to Molly. As she's only going back to work part time, now that her stomach ulcer is clearing up nicely, she's more than happy to come and look after Elizabeth here for a few days a week. I'll just be across the road so I can come home for feeds. We'll cut my clinic down from five days to two and a half. Donna will pick up any urgent patients and I'll do the house calls where, for the most part, I can take Elizabeth with me.'

He listened intently to what she was saying, feeling obsolete and unwanted. 'You have been busy.'

CJ realised Elizabeth was sound asleep and stood to put the baby in her nearby crib. One of her patients had made it for her and had even put wheels on the base so she could easily wheel it from room to room.

'Do you want me leave?' Ethan asked. 'Really want me to go?'

'Do you want to go?' She shook her head. 'I don't want you to feel as though you're stuck here. You've pointed out before that Pridham isn't your home, that being here is just a temporary interlude for you.' And she couldn't be the romantic lead in that interlude. It didn't work that way. 'You've told me you miss surgery.'

'Even if I return to Sydney, I won't be allowed to practise at the hospital. I'm on an enforced sabbatical, remember.'

'Oh, yeah.' She frowned. 'The last thing we need is for your stress level to go through the roof again.'

'Then me moving out of your home is the most obvious solution to our present dilemma.' He stood and looked down at the sleeping babe, knowing he would miss her a lot. It was quite incredible the way that holding the baby in his arms had not only helped to keep his stress level under control but had also helped him become reconciled with the loss of his own child. Seeing Elizabeth laugh and cry and pull all sorts of other funny faces had helped him to imagine what Ellie *might* have been like if she'd had the chance. But where Elizabeth de-stressed him, being so near to, so close to her mother had a completely different effect.

'Is being near Elizabeth too difficult for you?' CJ asked.

'No. Not Elizabeth.'

'Ah. Being near *me* is difficult.'

'Well, of course it is, CJ.' He raked a hand through his hair in total frustration. 'I can't be in the same room as you without wanting to drag you into my arms. I want to talk to you, spend time with you, see more of the countryside with you. Then reality sets in and I realise this isn't where I belong. I have work, CJ, important work back in Sydney.'

'That's your existence, Ethan. Where's your real life? The happiness?'

He turned and looked out the window into the dark night. He was silent for so long she didn't think he was going to answer. She was just about to leave when he said softly, 'I don't know.'

The emotions she felt for him rose up and overflowed. Slowly, she walked towards him and wrapped her arms around his waist. He tensed but when she didn't move, he shifted slightly so they were facing each other. They held each other, both content just to be. Ethan had never felt comfort like this before, never felt so calm and peaceful.

How long they stood there neither of them were sure but in the end CJ's yawn broke the moment.

'I'll think about whether I want to break the contract,' he stated softly. 'I'm just not sure.'

'OK. If you want to move out, I completely understand. You were never really comfortable here in the first place.'

'I like it here.' He looked down into her face, gazing at her lips. 'I like it too much. That's now the problem.'

'I know.' She waited for a moment, watching

him intently. 'It's crazy, isn't it…this thing between us?'

'Yes.' Ethan pulled superhuman strength from somewhere and gently released her from his arms. 'It's so…real. So powerful and intense.'

'Yes—but we can't, Ethan. *I* can't.'

He shook his head. 'Wait—why can't we, CJ? Tell me why?'

'Why? Because soon you'll be gone, Ethan. At the end of your time here, you'll head back to Sydney to your work. I'm not in that picture, and although I'd love nothing better than to be with you, it wouldn't work out—for many reasons.'

'This isn't just about me leaving, CJ. I know it's going to be hard for you to trust someone after Quinten and that's quite normal but I had hoped…that somehow I'd be able to show you not all men are lying cheats.'

'I understand that, Ethan, but—'

'Have I shown you that? Do you think that you could trust me?'

Ethan stood at the door to the lounge room, facing her—like a showdown at high noon. CJ didn't need this kind of questioning, didn't want to be put on the spot, and she certainly wasn't sure she could give him a direct answer. She glanced down at the floor before slowly returning to meet his gaze.

'Yes,' she said softly. 'Yes I think…in time… I could trust you, Ethan, and that fact alone scares me to death.' She bit her lip as it quivered, her eyes as wide as saucers—wearing her heart on her sleeve. 'I could trust you, I *do* trust you— to a certain extent, and even that has surprised me. I trust you one hundred percent in a professional capacity, I trust you with Elizabeth...' She smiled as she said her daughter's name. 'You're so good with her, so natural.'

'And do you trust me with *you*?'

The smile slipped away and CJ felt the tears threatening behind her eyes, felt her throat constrict as she desperately tried to swallow. 'I don't know if I'm strong enough to do that,' she whispered—a tear escaping and sliding slowly down her cheek. 'If I take the risk, if I give you my heart then I... I...' She shook her head, unable to continue.

'It's all right.' He wanted to go to her. He wanted it so badly and he could tell she wanted him to hold her but both of them stood their ground. 'It was a foolish question to have asked in the first place. Goodnight. I'll let you get some sleep while Elizabeth's sleeping.'

Ethan turned and stalked to the bathroom, stripping off his clothes. He turned on the taps and stepped beneath the spray, willing the water to soothe his aching muscles. At least he could do something about the physical aches he was feeling.

Why had it cut him straight to the heart when

she'd been unable to answer that question? She was right! He was leaving in five months' time to return to his life in Sydney and the uncontrollable chemistry that existed between them would wither and die when he left.

He scrubbed shampoo into his hair and rinsed it. Things between the two of them had gone too far, too fast and now they were both thoroughly confused. He wrenched off the taps and towelled himself dry.

Once he was dressed, he swallowed some paracetamol and settled down to work. Even though it was close to three o'clock in the morning, there was no way he'd be able to sleep now.

It was a few hours later that Ethan heard Elizabeth's cries come through the house. The little girl certainly had a good set of lungs. A moment later she was quiet and he knew CJ would be feeding her.

It brought back visions of CJ holding the baby tenderly in her arms, her manner natural and relaxed as Elizabeth fed greedily at first and then slowed down to a more sedate pace as her little tummy was filled. It was a sight that had touched him very deeply inside, in a secret place of longing he hadn't known existed.

The fact that he was in love with Elizabeth was of little doubt. 'And what about her mother?' he whispered into the dark.

* * *

The next day, CJ headed to the clinic to pick up her medical bag and the list of patients from Tania. Ethan came out to the waiting room while she was there.

'What are you doing here?' He looked around her. 'Where's Elizabeth?'

'At home with Molly. She's going to look after Lizzie while I do a few house calls.' CJ smiled politely at Ethan, picked up the medical bag and headed out the door, leaving him to watch her walk away. This has to be done, she kept reminding herself. She couldn't rely on him, not for anything. Although they'd talked, no firm decisions had been made and CJ needed to move forward, albeit slowly.

As she drove herself around the countryside, her anxiety at whether she was making the right choices started to wane. The scenery really was beautiful out here and after she'd seen three of her patients, she headed to Margaret's house to see how she was progressing.

CJ climbed the stairs and rang the doorbell. No answer. 'Margaret?' she called. 'It's CJ.' She rang the doorbell a few more times then headed around the large house to the back gate. Margaret's car was there but Doug's wasn't. At the back gate CJ was met by a large, barking dog but when she stepped through, the dog sniffing her and clearly recognising her, it started running off, almost stopping and waiting for her to follow. CJ's senses started tingling as apprehension washed over her. She headed around to the large glass back door, which, when she tried to slide the door open, she was pleased to find unlocked. The dog bounded inside and into the front lounge room. As CJ followed, she saw Margaret lying on the floor. Putting her bag down, she rushed to Margaret's side and pulled her phone from her pocket at the same time.

'Ambulance,' she stated as soon as the call was answered. She checked Margaret's pulse. It was there. 'Margaret! Margaret!' she called, but received no answer. CJ finished speaking to the ambulance service then called the clinic, alerting Ethan to the situation.

'I'll notify the hospital. How much has she had to drink?'

'I have no idea.'

'We'll need to do a blood alcohol test so we know what we're dealing with.'

'Can you organise the police?'

'Yes.'

'I'll call you from the ambulance,' she said. 'Can you have Tania notify Doug, please?'

'What about Margaret's parents?' Ethan asked.

'Let's just find Doug first.' When CJ ended the call, she continued to monitor Margaret's situation, her heart filled with concern not only for the woman but for the unborn child. As CJ did an assessment on Margaret's condition, constantly calling to the woman, trying to rouse her, she realised Margaret's jeans were wet…very wet. Her waters had broken.

By the time the ambulance arrived, CJ had managed to rouse Margaret once or twice, as well as find far too many empty wine bottles nearby. When the ambulance pulled up at the hospital, Ethan opened the back doors.

'Doug's on his way in,' he confirmed, as they wheeled Margaret through to the treatment room and transferred her to the hospital bed. Ethan was giving orders left and right.

'I want a blood test taken. Test for blood alcohol level and liver damage. Urine test as well to check for protein. How's her BP?' Bonnie and several of the nurses were carrying out the requests. Ethan strapped a foetal heart monitor to Margaret's abdomen in order to monitor the baby more closely.

Bonnie finished taking Margaret's blood pressure. 'Two hundred over one-ten.'

'Pregnancy-induced hypertension?' CJ checked and Ethan nodded. Margaret's blood pressure was high because she was in labour. She turned to Bonnie. 'Call Charlie and have him come in to assess her. I don't know if he can give her an epidural until we know her blood alcohol level so get a rush on that. Ethan, status on the baby?'

'Heart rate is still low but holding steady for the moment.'

'Good.'

The police arrived soon after and took statements from CJ, as well as doing their own blood alcohol test.

'Has she had any contractions?' Ethan asked.

'Not that I know of,' CJ answered.

'The alcohol might be acting as an anaesthetic so she may not be feeling them,' Ethan added. 'We're going to need to monitor that closely as well.'

CJ nodded and walked to the nurses' station, unable to believe how bad things had gone for Margaret. She closed her eyes for a moment and sighed, wondering if there couldn't have been more done for Margaret and the baby, but apart from forcing her to be hospitalised CJ wasn't sure Margaret had wanted their help.

'Are you OK?' Ethan's soft voice washed over her and she shook her head.

'GPs need to be better informed,' she said softly. 'We need to know what to look for, we need more seminars on these sorts of things—especially for those of us in rural or country areas. We're the first point of contact and we're the ones who usually look after the patients on a day-today basis.' She opened her eyes and turned to face him. 'We need to be better informed.'

Ethan listened to what she had to say. She was right. There was a lot of information in hospitals and city centres but they needed to broaden their horizons. 'You've raised a good point, CJ.' He'd been looking for a new research project and although it wasn't strictly his speciality, he knew several colleagues who could help him out. 'I'll see what I can do. In the meantime, don't go beating yourself up over Margaret.'

'Easier said than done. I've known her for years and although we've never been close friends, she was still a patient of mine and I'll always feel like I failed her.'

Ethan wanted to go to her, to stop her pain, to stop her hurting, but he knew he couldn't. To touch CJ, even in a gesture of comfort, wouldn't get them anywhere. He'd hold her and he'd want to keep her there. He'd want to kiss her, to let her know that he was there and that he really did care.

'I feel your frustration.'

She nodded as she remembered that this couldn't be at all easy for him either, given what had happened with his wife. 'I know you do.' Her smile encompassed him and immediately his heart, which had started to feel tight and con-stricted again, began to relax. What was it about her that enabled him to let go of his stress so easily?

'How's Elizabeth?'

'When I last checked with Molly, she was sleeping soundly.'

'Good.' He jerked his thumb over his shoulder. 'I'm going to go check on Margaret again. I think we need to get her transferred to the labour room.'

'OK. I'll wait here for Doug and bring him through. He shouldn't be too much longer.' Ethan nodded at her words, then headed off to oversee Margaret's transfer.

Three hours later, Margaret's blood alcohol level was reasonable enough for Charlie to attempt an epidural. She had started to feel the contractions, which was a good sign, but Ethan wasn't happy with the baby's present situation.

'Deceleration on the CTG. The baby's going into distress.' They shared a look and with a nod CJ turned to Charlie.

'Give me an epidural block, stat.'

The anaesthetist nodded and set to work.

'Bonnie,' CJ said, 'prep her for an emergency C-section and get the theatre ready.'

'What? What's going on?' Doug asked.

'The baby's not coping,' CJ explained.

'Not coping with what?'

'With everything. First of all, Margaret's blood

alcohol level when she came in was point one five. That's three times the state limit for driving.'

'But she's been drinking wine all her life. She can handle it.'

'*She* might be able to but the baby can't. Alcohol in the mother's blood crosses over to the baby through the placenta so the baby has the same blood alcohol level as Margaret. We've been over this several times with you, Doug!' CJ was feeling incredibly frustrated.

'What…what needs to happen now?'

'The baby is in distress, Doug. We need to get the baby out as soon as possible and Margaret's blood pressure keeps climbing. Both are in danger of losing their lives if we don't act immediately.'

He paled at her words. While she'd been talking, they'd been getting Margaret ready to move to the theatre. Once everything was ready, they wheeled her bed down, the machines and monitors she was hooked up to coming along beside the bed.

Soon Margaret was settled on the operating table with a screen erected around her shoulders to shield her from the operation. Ethan talked over the procedure with CJ while they scrubbed.

'Are you happy to take the lead?' she asked him.

'It's been a while since I've done a C-section but I did read up on it a few weeks ago to refresh my memory, just in case this eventuality presented itself.'

She nodded. 'And I've been reading up on what to do with the baby, just in case.'

'So have I.'

'Good. Then between the two of us we should be fine.'

Once Charlie had given Margaret the block, CJ and Ethan stepped up to the table. It wasn't long after making the incision that they were able to get the baby out.

'Congratulations,' CJ said, holding the baby up so Margaret and Doug could see.

'A boy!' Doug whooped. Margaret merely closed her eyes as though in pain. 'We're going to call him Joshua. Joshua Douglas,' Doug continued, a bright smile beaming across his face.

'That's a lovely name,' CJ replied.

Ethan was standing beside her, waiting with a warmed, sterile nappy in which to wrap the premature baby. CJ placed the little boy into Ethan's waiting hands. 'Forceps,' she said, and clamped the cord off with two sets of forceps, cutting the cord in between.

Ethan took the baby to the neonate section trolley, Bonnie working beside him. CJ delivered the placenta before starting to suture. 'How's it going?' she asked.

Ethan was rubbing the baby with one hand,

stimulating blood flow. 'Heart rate is low, breathing isn't too good. Bonnie, suction.'

Bonnie did as he asked while he checked the baby's reflexes and colour. 'Still quite blue. Come on, little man, come on,' he urged. He shook his head. 'We'll need to intubate. Facial features are indicative of FAS. Flat mid-face, low nasal bridge, indistinct philtrum and thin upper lip.'

'One minute,' Bonnie said.

'Apgar score is five,' Ethan remarked.

'What…what's going on?' Doug asked.

'The baby's not responding too well,' CJ said quietly. 'How are you doing, Margaret?'

There was no reply. CJ looked over the screen at her patient and saw tears running down the woman's cheeks.

'Blood pressure has stabilised,' Charlie reported, and CJ nodded.

'Colour is mildly improving,' Ethan called. 'Still clinical evidence of neurological dysfunction.'

'What does that mean?' Doug asked, looking worried.

'His reflexes aren't responding well,' CJ interpreted as he sutured Margaret's wound closed. Everyone was waiting.

'Five minutes,' Bonnie said.

'Apgar score is four,' CJ reported.

'What is this Ap thing?' Doug asked frantically.

'It's a score we use to assess the state of well-being in newborn babies.' CJ said.

'What's it out of?'

'Ten.'

'So...so four isn't good?'

'No.' Now was not the time to lie to them, to tell them everything would be all right—because it probably wouldn't. CJ's heart turned over with sympathy and pain for the new parents and she couldn't help her eyes misting with tears. She blinked them away and concentrated on her work.

'Arrange transfer for both Margaret and Joshua to Royal Sydney Children's Hospital,' Ethan said. He continued to monitor the baby and Margaret continued not to say anything. CJ could almost *feel* the guilt radiating from her patient and wished there was something she could do to help.

When it was time to transfer them, Ethan insisted on going with them.

'I can call in favours, get them the best care,' he told her.

CJ nodded. 'Keep me informed,' she said, watching him climb into the Royal Flying Doctor Service plane.

'I will,' he said, then disappeared from her view. She had no idea when he'd be able to return to Pridham, or even if he would. Once he was back in Sydney, perhaps he'd stay for a while. She didn't know. They hadn't had time to talk, to discuss things because she'd been busy trying to be independent and solve all her problems by herself.

If she'd just talked to him, been open and honest as she'd always prided herself on being, then perhaps she wouldn't be faced with so many questions. She headed home to Elizabeth, the house uncommonly quiet once Molly had left. CJ sat in the chair as she nursed her child, tears falling silently down her cheeks as she finally admitted the truth of the situation to herself.

She was in love with Ethan. Hopelessly, one hundred percent in love with him. And now he was gone.

CHAPTER THIRTEEN

THAT EVENING, by the time he'd handed over Margaret and baby Joshua's care to his colleagues, some of whom having been there during his own darkest hours, Ethan decided it was better for him to stay the night in Sydney. He took a taxi to St Aloysius Hospital and called CJ to give her an update. She must have been on another call as he ended up getting her voicemail.

'It's late, so I'll stay the night at my apartment in Sydney and will give you an update on the patients in the morning. I've asked the hospital to call me should there be any complications tonight, but when I left, things were stable. Joshua still isn't doing too well but at least they've managed to stabilise him, giving Margaret and Doug a bit more time with him. Er...yeah. So that's about it.'

Once he'd made that call, the next one he made was to Melody. She answered on the third ring.

'Dr Janeway.'

'Hello, Dr Janeway, this is the other Dr Janeway.'

'Ethan. How are things?'

'A bit crazy.' He raised his hand and knocked on an office door.

'Why? Oh, hang on a second,' Melody said. 'There's someone at my door.' She opened it and nearly screamed with delight when she saw him standing there. He disconnected the call and put his phone back in his pocket as his sister threw her arms around him. 'What are you doing here?'

Ethan quickly explained the situation and also that he needed the spare set of keys she had to his apartment. Melody instantly took them off her key-ring and handed them to him.

'How do you feel?'

'About?'

'About seeing another baby with FAS. Did it bring back memories of Ellie?'

'Everything brings back memories of Ellie. Every baby I see, every morning when I get up and feel that something is missing from my life.' He thought about the past few weeks, when he'd been able to wake in the mornings and hold Elizabeth in his arms. The sense of completion, of healing he'd had from having that little baby close to him had been a therapy he'd never anticipated.

'What are you thinking about now?'

'Elizabeth.' His smile was natural as he spoke the baby's name.

'CJ's daughter?'

'Yes.'

'You don't talk much about CJ,' Melody pointed out. 'I have a theory about that.'

He raised an eyebrow in her direction. 'Really? I can't wait to hear this one.'

'I think you're secretly infatuated with CJ because she's been able to help you get closure on your past.'

'Uh-huh. Anything else, Dr Freud?'

'Yes. I think Elizabeth has filled a void in your life and that's as clear as anything when you speak of her. Your face lights up and your entire demeanour changes. Your muscles relax and your eyes twinkle and you're…happy. I haven't seen you happy in so long, big brother, and the thing that scares me is what will happen when you leave Pridham and return to Sydney at the end of your contract. What happens when you've spent the past five and a half months becoming attached to a gorgeous little girl who doesn't belong to you?'

She wasn't saying anything he hadn't already asked himself, but at the moment he didn't have any answers.

'That little baby tonight—Joshua is his name— did bring back memories of Ellie, but this time, when I thought of her, I imagined her differently. I imagined her smiling at me and giggling and—' Ethan shook his head and tried again. 'It was as though I was imagining what she *would* have been like if she'd been born healthy.'

'Like Elizabeth?'

'Yes.'

'And Abigail? Have you been able to let go of your guilt?'

He nodded slowly. 'I think I'm getting there.' Ethan reached over and took his sister's hand in his. 'Thank you, Mel, for insisting I take a sabbatical, that I take the locum post in Pridham. You said it would be good for me to unwind, to unplug from the stress of the city, and you were right. I'm not saying there aren't stresses in Pridham, of course there are, but…taking a step back from the life I'd been living and being able to see how someone else lives their life has been a privilege.'

'You're talking about CJ's life?'

'Yes.' He smiled as he thought of her and breathed in deeply, filling his lungs completely. 'She relaxes me.'

'I see. CJ and Elizabeth relax you.'

'They do. They really do.'

'And what about the rest of Pridham?'

'It's very picturesque. Great to drive around in my car. CJ loves it.'

'She likes your car?'

He chuckled at that. 'She's a vintage car enthusiast herself.'

'Well…that is surprising. Clearly you two have a lot in common.'

'We do.'

Melody's phone rang and she quickly answered it, sighing heavily as she listened to her registrar. 'Sorry, Ethan,' she stated after disconnecting the call. 'Emergency. I've gotta go.'

'That's fine.' He stood and hugged her close. 'Hey, what's happening with the directorship for Orthopaedics?'

Melody bit her lip, then pointed to herself. Ethan's eyes widened with surprise. 'You're taking it?'

'Acting Head of Orthopaedics at your service.' She gave a little bow. 'Don't know how I got talked into it, but it'll only be temporary, I tell you that much.' They stepped outside her office and she locked the door. 'Anyway, how long are you planning on being in Sydney?'

'I'm not sure. It depends on Joshua. Probably a day or two.'

'OK. So I can see you before you head back to the country?'

'Sure.' He walked her down to the emergency department, being stopped by several people on the way to shake hands and say hello, but then they were off again, busy, busy, busy. After Melody had left, Ethan looked around the ED. People everywhere, everyone hectic and overworked. It was as though he felt the stress the place exuded and when he tried to take a breath, it was odd that he couldn't quite fill his lungs.

He closed his eyes, thought of CJ's smile and the way Elizabeth felt snuggled into his arms.

Then he breathed in again, all the way, and felt the stress of his past life melt away as he exhaled.

Returning to his apartment, he was shocked at the stark contrast of the minimalist furnishings compared to CJ's comfortable and homely house. Here there were no pictures on the walls of cars or people, no solid jarrah desks in the corner or comfortable bed linen on beds. Everything here was utilitarian and practical. That was the state his life had been in prior to heading to Pridham, prior to meeting CJ.

He took out his phone and went to call her again but on checking the time he realised it was too late. He didn't have anything to report on their patients and if she'd managed to get Elizabeth to sleep, there was no way he was going to disturb any shut-eye she might actually get.

Where did he live? CJ had asked him that question and he hadn't been able to answer her. Now, looking around his apartment, he at least had part of the answer to that question. 'I don't live here any more.'

By the time he flew back to Pridham and managed to arrange for someone to pick him up from the airstrip and drive him into town, it was well into the evening. He'd ended up being in Sydney for three days, monitoring the conditions of Margaret and Joshua, talking to several people about the possibility of a new research project with FAS, and having lunch with his sister.

When he headed to the back door of the house, he once again found it unlocked and shook his head. Didn't CJ realise she was a mother now, that she needed to lock the doors in order to protect both herself and Elizabeth from harm? Of course, CJ would just counter anything he said with her statistics that Pridham had practically no crime and that if people were going to get into the house, they might smash a window, which would cause more injury and damage than an unlocked door. Her argument was a valid one and a part of him was pleased that she did live in a place where crime was low and Elizabeth could grow up enjoying being part of a close-knit community.

As he went through the house, he listened for sounds of CJ and Elizabeth, unable to believe just how much he'd missed the two of them. They were so vitally important to him and he'd come back to tell CJ as much. To share with her the decisions he'd made and to ask her opinion. He valued her opinions, he valued *her*. Would she be able to value him?

'Hello?' he called softly as he headed into the lounge room. It was empty. He went towards CJ's part of the house and knocked softly on the door. 'Hello?' he called again, and pushed open the door. 'CJ?' He'd tried calling her from the airstrip to let her know he was back but again his call had gone through to her voicemail. Had she got the message?

'Ethan? Is that you? Because if it's not and you're a robber, there's absolutely nothing of value in the house. Just boring memorabilia, which won't fetch you any money if you sell it on the internet.'

He grinned at her words, following the sound of her voice to the bedroom. The door was open and he stopped on the threshold, looking at her standing over Elizabeth's crib, the baby sound asleep. She was dressed in a pair of pyjamas with her robe belted firmly around her waist. He glanced down at her feet and wasn't surprised to see those fluffy slippers she loved so much. At first he'd thought they were ridiculous, but now he realised they suited her. They reflected her personality—warm, soft and comfortable. She probably wouldn't like to hear herself being described that way—what woman would? But Ethan had never felt as comfortable in his life as he did when he was with CJ.

'You're back,' she whispered with a sigh of relief.

'I did leave you a message.' He pointed to her phone, which was on her bedside table.

She nodded. 'I got it. So... Joshua's finally

picked up?' She bit her lip and shook her head as tears began to well in her eyes.

'A little,' he confirmed. 'Margaret and Doug have a very long road ahead of them, one that will take years to adjust to. The full extent of Joshua's brain damage is unknown as yet but he'll need to be in hospital for at least the next six months.' He broke off and shook his head. 'Margaret's already talking about selling their share of the vineyard and moving to Sydney.'

'She is?'

Ethan nodded. 'She says she, Doug and Joshua need a new start, one away from her parents.'

'Huh. Good for Margaret.'

'Sometimes when we face our worst fears, we become stronger,' he said as he crossed the room to stare down into Elizabeth's crib, putting his arm around CJ's waist. 'I'm glad Joshua didn't die because the death of a child is…heartbreaking and soul-destroying. It can take years of therapy, of working through things, of having a complete change of scenery, before something clicks and life starts making sense again.'

She knew he was talking about himself, as well as the very long road forward that both Doug and Margaret would face.

'You faced your fears when you were left alone and pregnant and now…' He gestured to Elizabeth. 'Look at that gorgeous girl.'

'She's stolen my heart.' As CJ spoke, her emotions welled and tears pricked at her eyes.

'Mine, too.'

'I love her so much, Ethan. I never knew I could love someone that much before. I certainly never loved Quinten like this.'

'It's a mother's love.'

'It's a parent's love,' she said as she leaned into him further. 'And I'm still scared. I'm scared I'm going to let her down in the future, I'm scared I'm going to make mistakes, I'm scared that there are so many things that can go wrong. I don't want her to skin her knee falling off her bike. I don't want her to be teased in school. I don't want her have her heart broken when she's older. I want only the best.' CJ's emotions bubbled up and over.

'Oh, CJ.' He ground out her name and in an instant he'd gathered her closer to him. He knew her emotions were that of a person who desperately cared about her patients, not only their medical issues but their personal ones as well. Added to that was the fact that she'd not long given birth herself. He knew she'd be thinking about how she would feel should something terrible happen to Elizabeth. Even as the thought passed through his mind, he felt a surge of empowered protectiveness fill him completely. Elizabeth was vitally important to him, she'd become a part of him and he loved her. If anything were to happen to her…

CJ pulled back slightly, sniffing and rummaging in her robe pocket for a tissue. She blew her nose and looked up at him, overcome with love when she saw tears glistening in his eyes.

'I couldn't bear it if anything happened to our Lizzie…or to you.' He shook his head. 'I missed you both, so much.'

'Missed us?'

'In Sydney. I slept in a sterile, bland apartment. I chatted with people in the hospital corridors for all of thirty seconds because they were always busy going somewhere or doing something, having no time for real discussions or connections. My world there is…empty, and it's empty because *you* and our gorgeous Elizabeth aren't in it.'

She couldn't believe what she was hearing. It was what she'd been dreaming about, desperate to hear him say that he wanted to stay, that he wanted to be with her. She knew he'd suffered terrible pain but surely he could see that he was just the type of man who deserved to be loved? She loved him. Loved him desperately and she wanted him to know that, to understand that she would do everything she could to make him happy, to make his heart smile once more, to shine her whacky brand of sunshine into his life—for ever. She wanted to tell him, she was bursting to tell him, but would he...could he...really feel the same? Was she hoping for too much? There was only one thing to do—she needed to ask him.

'But here?' The words were soft yet held the strongest thread of hope. 'In Pridham? H-how does your world look here?' Even after she'd spoken, she tried not to hold her breath. This was the moment. What he said now might make her the happiest woman in the world...or... No. She wouldn't even contemplate what that 'or' might mean. Swallowing over the nervous lump in her throat, it seemed for ever before he spoke.

Ethan's smile was bright and filled with hope. 'Here...' He gazed into her eyes and her heart turned over with a new wave of love for this incredible and wonderful man. 'Here, my life is in technicolor.'

'Really?' Hope flared higher.

'Yes. It's so vibrant and alive that I need to wear sunglasses.'

CJ laughed joyously at his words. Ethan loved being here...with her.

'You once asked me where my life was and at the time I didn't know.' His gaze hovered momentarily on her mouth, her lips parted and quivering with anticipation. 'I do now. I know where my life is, CJ.' He looked deeply into her eyes before he continued, his words filled with absolute certainty, 'My life…is with *you*. You and Elizabeth. You're my everything.'

A flood of delighted tingles spread throughout CJ's entire body, giving the hope wings that soared to its fullest glory. 'Oh, Ethan,' she breathed, her voice catching on the words. Elation and utter happiness continued to tingle their way around her.

'I know this may seem sudden or crazy or both but…' He stopped and forced himself to slow down. 'I know you've been hurt so badly in the past but I promise I will accept you for the incredibly intelligent, vivacious, honest and hardworking person you are. I trust you, CJ, I trust you with my heart. I give it to you, now and for ever.' He took a deep breath and then slowly exhaled. 'I love you, Claudia-Jean.'

'You… You…' She couldn't get the words out. Her mind was trying desperately to compute everything he'd been saying and the whole time he'd been talking her heart had been singing with delight.

'I love you,' he said for her, and placed a firm kiss on her mouth, as though desperate to prove his point. The kiss instantly turned hard, possessive and urgent. He was a man dying of thirst in the desert and finally finding water. He pulled back and tenderly caressed her cheek. 'I love you,' he stated again, then chuckled. 'I can't believe how many times I'm saying it. I can't seem to stop.'

'Don't ever stop,' she instructed. 'Always reassure me that you love me.' As she said the words, he heard the quiver in her voice, saw the pain, the hurts, the betrayals of the past. She was scared but he knew he could fix it.

'I promise to tell you every day—even if we're having an open and honest disagreement—that I love you. I could *never* want another woman, CJ, because you're all I need. Well…you and Elizabeth.' He laughed. 'The two of you have brought me back to life and I can never thank you enough for opening your life and letting me in. I know you're scared and you have every right to be but you must feel how different things are this time.'

'Yes. It's *very* different. Before you went to Sydney, I wasn't sure if I could trust you with my heart but when you weren't here, not only was the house so dark and lonely, my life was dark and lonely.' She pulled back to look at him. 'You're right. I'm scared. I'm scared to take another chance at love, at marriage—especially as I have Elizabeth to think about this time—but I'm even *more* scared to live my life without you.' Her lower lip trembled. 'Oh, Ethan. I need you so much.'

Ethan couldn't stand it any more. He crushed her to him once again and pressed his mouth to hers. She was his—and he was *never* letting her go. She and Elizabeth were his family. His heart had known it for a while but his mind had taken a little while to catch up.

Eventually, he released her and she smiled up at him. 'I still can't believe you're really here.'

'I am and I'm never leaving you again. I must have been mad.'

'You're really staying? Here? In Pridham?'

'If you'll marry me.'

'Married? Are you sure?'

'One hundred percent. My life is…meaningless without you.' He paused and stared into her eyes, showing her every aspect of his vulnerabilities. 'Please, CJ? Marry me. Be my partner for life. We'll love our Lizzie and we'll love any other children we might have.'

'You want more children?'

'I do. I really do. I want to fill this house with fun and laughter and noise.' He paused, sadness creeping into his words. 'I'll always love Ellie, and Abigail, but they were my past. *You* are my future. You and Lizzie-Jean. I love you. Will you? Will you marry me?'

CJ's heart overflowed with love for the man before her. 'Yes. Oh, yes, yes, yes. I need you, Ethan Janeway. I need you and I trust you.' She placed her hand on his cheek. 'In fact, I adore you.' She kissed him again, then drew back with a gasp. 'But what about your job in Sydney? What will you do here?'

'Firstly, I've resigned from the hospital.'

'What?'

'Secondly, I've decided to set up a private practice here, in Pridham. A permanent general surgeon for the Pridham and Whitecorn district hospitals. Also, I've started negotiations for my next research project, which will be a collaboration with a few of my colleagues at the Royal Sydney Children's Hospital.'

'FAS?'

'Yes, and no doubt we'll be wanting your input, too.'

'Really? I get to have my name on a published paper?' She giggled. 'This really is a night of dreams coming true.' CJ sighed, content and happy and amazed that she could feel this good.

Elizabeth shifted beneath her covers, sniffling a little before starting to cry. Ethan released CJ and bent to pick the baby up. 'That cry doesn't sound good. Is she all right?'

'She's been a little unsettled for the past few days.'

'What?' He picked her up and kissed her forehead. 'Are you all right, my darling?'

CJ's heart melted at the way he genuinely loved their Lizzie. 'She'll be fine…now.'

'Now?'

'We've both been a little unsettled for the past few days. We've been fretting.'

'Fretting?'

'Over you.'

His concerned look disappeared as he held out his other arm to CJ. 'Come here.' He held her close. 'You'll never have to fret again. Either of you. We're a family and we'll be sticking together for ever.' Then Ethan kissed her in such an intense and passionate way that she knew their love *would* last for ever.

The baby slept on.

EPILOGUE

THE WEDDING WAS the most glorious day of her life. The night before she'd insisted on spending the night at Donna's place while Ethan had stayed at her home—*their* home now. They'd made plans to alter the renovations that CJ had not long finished but as both of them enjoyed renovating and restoring old things, it would be a challenge they could do together.

Ethan, as well as covering CJ's clinics, had already started his own general surgical practice. Consulting at both Pridham and Whitecorn hospitals, his clinics booking up so fast he thought he might need to add an extra day in the future. For now, though, he was more than happy playing Mr Mum while CJ eased herself back into part-time consulting. They both enjoyed their days at home with Lizzie-Jean and doing things together as a family at weekends.

'Are you sure you're happy?' CJ had asked Ethan a few days ago.

'I'll be happier when you're legally my wife.' He'd hauled her close and kissed her soundly. 'I love you so much, CJ.' He'd laughed with such carefree abandon that any minor concerns she'd harboured had vanished. 'I can't believe how incredible I feel being here, with you and our Lizzie-Jean and the people of the community.' Ethan had shaken his head in bemusement. 'I never thought I'd say it but... I'm glad I had that minor heart attack.'

CJ had shuddered at the mention of it. 'I'm not.'

'If I hadn't, I wouldn't have re-evaluated my life, I wouldn't have come here, I wouldn't have found you, I wouldn't be blessed with another family to love and cherish, for ever and ever, until death us do part.'

'Practising your vows?'

'I don't need to practise them. They're tat-tooed on my heart.'

And so when the time came for CJ to marry her beloved Ethan, the ceremony being held at Donna's small vineyard, her heart had been sure and confident. Ethan loved her. Ethan loved Lizzie-Jean. She loved Ethan and Lizzie-Jean... well, Lizzie-Jean seemed to love whoever was cuddling her. The little girl was a delight and one that had only enhanced the happiness CJ had thought she'd never feel.

As she stood facing Ethan, holding his hands and gazing into his eyes, while Lizzie-Jean slept on nearby in Aunty Melody's arms, CJ couldn't help but laugh.

'What's so funny?' Ethan stared at her and slowly shook his head, his own lips beginning to twitch. 'You're supposed to be saying your vows, not laughing.'

'But I'm just *so* happy.' She giggled again. '*You* make me so happy, Ethan. You came into my life when I needed you most—and then stayed. You stayed. I want you to know that I will always be here for you, that I will do my very best to always communicate with you, to share my thoughts, my feelings and my concerns with you. Good and bad. Happy and sad... But here's hoping it's mostly happy. I think we've both had enough sadness.'

'And I promise to do everything I can to keep that smile on your face, to keep that giggle bubbling up and your eyes shining with delight. I adore you, Claudia-Jean. I love you. My heart is yours for ever...except for the part we share with Lizzie-Jean—'

'And any other children we might have.'

Ethan nodded. 'We'll build a home filled with thoughtfulness, kindness, love, patience and—'

'And a thousand other good things,' she interjected once more.

'Will you let me finish?' he demanded, and a chuckle rippled through the crowd that was gathered around them, helping them celebrate this wonderful union.

'In a minute.' She leaned forward and kissed him firmly on the mouth.

'Uh... I haven't got to that bit yet,' the celebrant said, but no one seemed to mind.

CJ pulled back and looked at her beloved. 'I love you, Ethan Janeway.'

'I love you back,' he responded, then, after kissing her once more, he settled her a small way from him, his hands still firmly holding hers, and turned to the celebrant.

'OK. Get to the part where you pronounce us a family—because we've got some serious celebrating to do!'

The celebrant chuckled but did as she was bidden and a short while later CJ was officially Ethan's wife and Ethan was officially CJ's husband. And both of them were officially ready to start their new life together.

For ever.

* * * * *

Look out for the next great story in the
SYDNEY SURGEONS *duet*

ONE WEEK TO WIN HIS HEART

And if you enjoyed this story, check out these other great reads from Lucy Clark

THE FAMILY SHE'S LONGED FOR
REUNITED WITH HIS RUNAWAY DOC
ENGLISH ROSE IN THE OUTBACK
A FAMILY FOR CHLOE

All available now!